My Baby Loves the
Western Movies

THE LATE SHOW

By L. Z. Smith

From a story suggested by

Joshua S. Smith

Courage is of no value unless accompanied by justice; yet if all men became just, there would be no need for courage.

Agesilaus the Second

All characters depicted in this book are creations of the author. Any similarities with people living or dead are coincidental.

Global Talent Agency, LLC
a wholly owned subsidiary of
Global Artist Agency, LLC
2601 Magnolia Blvd. Suite 101.
Burbank, California 91505
Cover illustration by Nuria

LOCAL 4
PUBLISHING

Localfourpublishing@gmail.com

Chapter One

"Gradma, I killed the cow..."
-Waco

The water truck rolled along the highway, clearing its way through the spring downpour. Waco, the handsome seventeen year old driver, stared out the blurred windshield thinking how foolish it would seem to a man from outer space landing in the middle of the Arizona desert and seeing him delivering water in the middle of a rainstorm. But Waco knew that by morning the rain would be dried up and the blistering sun would soon crack the dirt and sand of the thirsty desert.

It made him feel important. Not only did the Southern Arizona Fresh Spring Water Company pay him for this out-of-the-way delivery, but he was also doing something for his own town of Norte del Sur. The fact was that if he didn't deliver the water every other Saturday, supplementing the old water tower, the company would drop the town from its route, despite the fact that it advertised, "We deliver fresh spring water anywhere, anytime." He wondered what they would do if someone in China were to order water from them. He wondered what would happen if he didn't deliver water to Norte del Sur and the small community across the border in Mexico that was also called Norte Del Sur. As far as the Southern Arizona Fresh Spring Water Company was concerned, along with a lot of other people in Southern Arizona, Norte del Sur could just as well dry up and blow away. The only reason he got the job if the first place was because no one else wanted it. The man who hired him said if he hadn't answered the ad in *Yuma Star* the company would have dropped Norte del Sur from their routes. So once every two weeks he caught a ride into Yuma and climbed into the old delivery truck for twenty bucks a haul and the satisfaction that he was doing a good thing for his town.

A streak of lightening disappeared into the golden glow of a giant setting sun that had dipped below the black rain clouds. A clap of thunder lazily rolled across the endless sky. The rainstorm had made him late. If he didn't hurry with his deliveries he would miss the evening movie on TV; John Wayne in "Rio Bravo". Everyone would be over at the Pass Time where Sid had a twenty-one inch black and white set. He could see them hovered around the TV; the old folks: Sid, Luke, Suzie, Mattie, and Bertha, and his friend Sarah, the only other young person left in Norte del Sur. Sarah was Mattie and Luke's granddaughter, but for Sarah all the old people of Norte del Sur were family, and when it got right down to it, they were the only family he had beside his grandma Poppy. There was no one else. "Where's Waco?" they'd say. "He never misses John Wayne."

He drove past Daisy's Diner. Tex's double trailer cattle rig was just pulling out from the dirt parking lot. He could hear the roar from the powerful Mack truck's diesel engine.

Tex liked killing rabbits and armadillos or anything else that strayed onto the highway. He kept a score board on the dash of the Mack truck—told Waco one time that it was best driving at night when the headlights of the truck mesmerized the animals that came onto the road for warmth. "Got more than a hundred in one run," he boasted.

But that wasn't the only reason Waco didn't like him. It was because Tex thought he owned the highway; him and his Mack truck. One of his favorites was driving up to the bumper of some old person, or a farmer in a loaded pickup and then blasting his horn, and scaring the hell out of them. Tex was just plain mean. So when Waco saw the Mack truck's headlights coming up in his rear view mirror, he pressed his Double Eagle cowboy boot down on the throttle. There was only four miles to the Norte del Sur turnoff and he would be damned if he was going to let Tex pass him. But the old water truck wasn't very fast, even with only ten water bottles loaded on it, and Tex bore down on him in no time. Waco heard the blast from the diesel horn, and saw the headlights of the Mack truck flash in his side view mirror as the truck swung out into the left lane to pass him. Waco swerved to block the big rig. His tires began to slide on the wet asphalt and he struggled to keep control. Tex blasted the horn again, only to have it drowned out by a crash of thunder as the sky lit up from a streak of lightening that struck in the middle of the highway in front of them. Waco pulled back into the right lane to counter a move by the Mack truck, and then swerved back into the center of the road. By now Tex just laid on his horn, blasting it as if he were competing with the thunder.

The sign reading Norte del Sur/Border Crossing appeared through the rain streaked windshield of the water truck, just as the Mack truck hit its rear bumper. For a moment Waco felt himself being pushed along by the powerful cattle carrier. He saw the turnoff onto the gravel road that led to Norte del Sur and tried to steer clear from the clutches of the Mack truck. But the big rig's diesel was too powerful and he felt himself skid sideways along the slippery highway.

The sky lit up and thunder boomed in his ears as he saw the side of the road coming at him. He no longer had any control. The last thing he saw was the desert in front of him and the faint shadow of a four legged animal appear out of the darkness as the water truck headed for a ditch off the shoulder of the road. He came to a jarring stop. He heard the diesel horn blaring and saw Tex's red tail lights as the Mack truck roared past and disappeared into the darkness.

The sound of raindrops pounded on the water truck and Waco knew that his engine had stalled out. He remembered the dull thud as he went into the ditch and figured he must have hit something. Then he remembered the shadow. He stepped out of the truck. Water poured off his wide brimmed hat. He was soaking wet from the pouring rain. Sweat poured down his narrow half shaven face. He made his way through the mud to the front of the truck to see what it was that he had hit.

It was dead for sure—his grandmother's cow. It was all that was left of their small ranch—the only livestock left that had made it worthwhile calling it a ranch, and while the cow hadn't been able to breed in five years, it had given his grandmother an excuse to stay on the small spread.

"Everyone may have given up on this place," she said, "but as long as we got live stock we got a ranch." And now the cow was dead. The front of the truck was smashed. Steam escaped from the radiator and drifted up into the cold rain. There was nothing to do but walk the quarter of a mile to the ranch and break the news to his grandmother. She'd want to know. The cow was only an excuse anyway. She'd never leave the ranch. She'd been there since 1910. She'd die there.

Chapter Two

"It's only TV, grandpop. It ain't real,"
-Joe

The old Indian sat on a blanket in front of the small screen black and white TV. The flickering light from the set lit up the windowless adobe walls of the one room house. Shadows played across the old man's face marked like deep map of the canyons and arroyos of the desert that had been his home for over eighty years. His large nose with sharp black eyes set close against it gave him the look of a hawk. His cobalt gray hair hung down over his broad shoulders in two long braids as he leaned in close to the TV screen. The sounds of a shoot-em-up Western echoed out into the starless night. In the corner of the room the old Indian's grandson, Joe, sat at a wooden table scanning a letter for the third time by the dim light of a kerosene lamp. He was his Grandfather sixty years younger with long shiny black hair and smooth bronze skin.

"Bull," the old Indian said. "This stuff is bull," talking to the TV set.

"It's only TV, grandpop. It ain't real," the boy mumbled, turning his sharp featured dark face to the old man.

"It bull," the old man repeated without letting his eyes stray from the small screen. "You read letter from your brother?"

The boy looked up from the paper to the old man, wondering how he knew the letter was from his older brother.

"Yes grandpop."

"When he come home?" the old man said, still keeping his eyes glued to the TV screen.

"He's out of the army," Joe said.

"He come home. He be chief. I can join our ancestors," the old man said.

"He's all right. He sends his regards."

"When he come home?"

Joe looked at the picture that accompanied the letter. It showed his brother, still in uniform with a fat blond white girl standing next to a new Chevy Camaro in front os a small tract house.

"He says..."

"When he come home!" the old Indian said again, his eyes never leaving the small flickering screen.

"He...he says he'll be home soon."

"Good," the old man said. "This John Wayne, him big phony. I think him bull. I think all TV bull."

"Why do you watch it, Grandpop?"

"Nothing better to do," the old man said.

A dog began to bark outside, announcing an in-

truder. Joe stood to up. His muscular body moved eas-
ily through the darkened room as he grabbed a shotgun on the way to the door. He carefully unlatched the
lock and swung the door open.

Waco stood there in the rain. Water poured off his
hat and rain poncho. He carried a cigar box tucked
under his arm.

"Waco, what're you doing here?"

"Grandma's dead," Waco said without moving. "I
smashed up the water truck, and grandma's dead."

"Oh shit, man. Come in out of the rain."

Waco stepped inside the house and took off his
pancho and hat. His long sandy blond hair was mat-
ted from the rain and the single pony tail trailed like a
wilted snake down his back. "What happened, man?"
Joe asked.

"Don't know. I got home and she was just dead,
that's all," Waco said. "Didn't know what to, so I sad-
dled up the old pinto and rode over here." His eyes
drifting to the TV set. "Rio Bravo. That's a good one."

"It bull," the old chief muttered.

"Sit down, man. I'll get you some coffee and a tow-
el."

"Got something stronger?"

"Sure man. Picked up a bottle Thunderbird this
morning."

Joe twisted opened the bottle of rose colored wine
and put it on the table. Waco sat down and put the cigar box next to the bottle. He picked the bottle up and
took a long drink. "Killed the cow, too," he said after
swallowing the cheap wine. It warmed his stomach.
"Must of got out. Grandma told me to fix the fence.

Now she's dead, and so's the cow."

"Jesus, man. You've had a bad night," Joe said.

Waco looked up at his friend and began to laugh. "A bad night?" he laughed. "Yeah." Suddenly everything seemed funny and the laughter eased the tension that had built up inside him since he smashed up the Water truck. His grandmother had been nearly a hundred years old. He had lived everyday expecting to find her dead. Now that it had happened it was almost a relief. He finally stopped laughing and took another drink from the Thunderbird bottle.

Joe looked at his friend. His people lived with misfortune daily. He could understand his friend's reaction. he took a drink from the bottle. "Well," he said. "What're you going to do now?"

"Got to take care of Grandma," Waco said, opening the lid of the cigar box.

He dumped the contents on the table. There were several faded medals, a rusty tin star, an envelope, yellowed from age, marked, "Open in case of death," and an old Colt .45 six-shooter wrapped in a red bandana.

Waco opened the envelope. "It has the address of a funeral parlor in Yuma."

"What are the medals?" Joe asked.

"Belonged to Grandpa Lemuel. Fought in the Spanish-American War...or was it the Civil War? Can't remember. Guess Grandma wanted to be buried with them."

Joe picked up the badge and read it. "Sheriff- Norte del Sur."

Waco picked up the gun and inspected it. Then he

stuck it in his belt. Joe handed him the badge and he put it in his pocket.

"Gotta borrow the truck, Joe. Gotta get grandma into Yuma."

"Sure man. I'll come with you."

"Thank's partner. Better pick up the water, too. Gotta deliver the water."

"Say, you kids pipe down," the old chief said. "Can't hear the TV."

"Poppy Merkins is dead," the Indian boy said.

"Huh?" the old man answered, keeping his eyes glued to the TV.

"Poppy Merkens. Sheriff Merkins widow." Joe repeated.

`"Poppy dead, eh. She pretty old. Time to join ancestors."

"Don't mind him," Joe said to Waco.

Waco just shrugged. His eyes drifted back to the John Wayne movie. He rested his hand on the old six-shooter in his belt.

Chapter Three

"He's got us. We're his family."
-Sarah

Joe's truck was not a truck at all but a World War II ambulance, complete with drab green paint and a red cross insignia on the side. It's four wheel drive and low gears made it a perfect desert vehicle.

The ambulance's large dirt tires kicked up the last mud from the rain storm the night before as it rolled across the dirt road into Norte del Sur. The hot morning sun was already rendering the landscape back to its naturally arid state.

Waco slouched down in the passenger seat so that only the brim of his hat stuck up over the window as the car radio blasted a Country Western song. Joe steered the ambulance down the dirty road lined with deserted wooden buildings that were slowly decaying. A tall wooden water tower dominated the area with NORTE DEL SUR, ARIZONA painted across it in fading letters.

A tall gray haired man stood precariously on a ladder with a paint brush, carefully touching up a faded sign announcing:

THE PASS TIME
All your needs under one roof
Ice Cold Beer
Sid's tours - inquire within
Tourist cabins

An 1955 Ford station wagon sat next to an ancient Model A touring car with "Sid's Wild West Tours" painted on the side along with an elaborate picture of an Indian on horseback shooting an arrow into a raging buffalo.

Joe blasted the horn of the ambulance, jarring the old man's attention from his project.

"Hey, Sid," Joe shouted. "Got your water."

Sid carefully came down the ladder and walked over to the ambulance where Waco continued to sit with his head down.

Despite his sixty-eight years Sid was still handsome. He had a full head of white hair and his face was a nutty brown from the desert sun that carved creases and lines which, in other men would have made them look old, but made him distinguished. His open western shirt exposed tufts of gray on a powerful chest.

"There you are, Waco. Expected you yesterday. Missed a great John Wayne picture. Say, where's the truck? " Sid said.

Joe got out of the ambulance and was at Sid's side. "Leave him be, Sid."

"What's the matter, you boys hit into that Thunderbird last night? How you kids can drink that crap I'll never know...why, when I was young..."

Joe took Sid by the arm, led him to the rear of the ambulance, and opened the back doors. There, tucked neatly between the water bottles lay Waco's grandmother's body, wrapped in a Indian blanket like a papoose.

"Oh, my God!...Poppy Merkins," Sid said, looking down at the body.

"Waco smashed up the water truck last night. We're dropping off the water and then taking her into Yuma to get her fixed up for burying," Joe said.

"My God," Sid said again, still looking down at the dead face. "Sure is dead alright. Never thought she'd be the first to go. Well, she had a full and rich life."

"Rich, my ass. All she owned was that sorry excuse of a ranch we live in."

Sid turned around. Waco was standing behind him. "Well. I meant rich...you know what I meant. God, Waco, we're all going to miss her."

"Yeah, I know," Waco said.

A girl's voice rang out from the porch of the Pass Time.

"Waco, where you been? Missed a great John Wayne movie last night. Everyone missed you."

Waco looked up as the young woman came down from the porch. Sarah's mature eighteen year old body lay hidden beneath a floppy flannel western style shirt. A bandana around her head covered long dirty reddish brown hair that framed her smooth sun tanned face.

"Quiet girl," Sid scolded. "Show some respect."

"What, for these two?" she snapped back, and then peeked into the back of the ambulance. "Oh." she whispered. "Is she dead?"

"Course she's dead," Sid said.

Sarah put her hand on Waco's. "Gee Waco, I'm sorry. We all loved Poppy."

Waco looked into the girls clear blue eyes. They had grown up together in Norte del Sur; both abandoned by their mothers when they were young. But suddenly he felt like he had never looked at her before. She had become I woman, and, for a brief moment, he felt shy and averted his eyes from hers. He had never had a hard time talking to her before, but now his words stuck in his throat. "I know you loved her, Sar. Thanks," he managed to say.

"Well Waco, guess you ain't got no family around here now," Sid said, putting his hand on Waco's shoulder.

"What do you mean, Uncle?" Sarah interrupted. "He's got us. We're his family."

"Yeah, sure. I meant blood...you know. Course, as long as me and the rest of us are here, you've got plenty of family, Waco. You know what I mean."

"Sure." Waco said with a half smile. "I know that, Sid."

Joe pulled five water bottles from the truck and put them on the porch. "We're taking her into Yuma, Sar. You coming?"

The girl looked at Waco. "I'd like to come along...if it's okay with you, Waco."

"Sure, I'd like that." he answered, rearranging the remaining water bottles around his grandmother's body.

"Where you think you're going, girl?" Sid said. "You've got chores around here. It's tourist season. Death may come, but life must go on..."

"Sure Sid, but I'd better go anyway. We're out of beans and Bromo Seltzer," Sarah said, knowing that the only tourists they were likely to see would be Bull Martin, the insurance salesmen who showed up every year to push funeral insurance on the old people.

"You're right! Plum forgot. I'll get Luke and the girls to help. Waco, son, don't worry about a thing. We'll take care of everything...the funeral I mean. Say, maybe this is a sign. I gotta feeling things is going to change around here. You know what I mean, good things coming out of tragedy...you know what I mean," Sid said, patting Waco on the back.

"Sure Sid," Waco said, suddenly feeling more sorry for the old man than for his grandmother or himself. "We'd best get going. Gotta stop at Mama Lo's before we head into Yuma."

The three teenagers piled into the ambulance.

Sid shook his head. "Poppy Merkins," he said to himself, shaking his head. "Guess it's up to me to break the news to Luke and the girls..."

Joe gunned the engine and ground the gears into low. The ambulance roared off down the street in the direction of the Mexican border.

"Luke..." Sid shouted as he headed back into the Pass Time.

Chapter Four

"All the gringos vamos when they ain't got nothing to keep them here.".

-Mama Low

The two guards sat at a table that straddled the international border. The one dressed in the starched uniform of the U.S. Immigration Service dealt from a deck of old cards to his counterpart on the Mexican side.

It was an easy post. Nothing ever happened at the Norte del Sur border crossing. Neither government cared enough for the desolate area to bother investing in any improvements, including paved roads. In fact, the road on the Mexican side leading to San Luis. the town just across the border from Yuma, had been washed out six months earlier and never reopened. Nothing happened there because there was nothing to happen.

Behind the Mexican guard was a row of deserted crumbling adobe buildings along the dirt road of the small community that no one had ever bothered to name, except to call it Norte del Sur for the town five miles on the north side of the border. The first of the buildings was the hub of the border settlement:

MAMA LO'S CAFE
Since 1890
Pancho Villa ate here

Behind it several adobe cottages lined another dirt road that lead to the washed out highway. A group of children played in the street as an old dog curled up in the shade next to one of the buildings. An old woman hung her wash on a line. The few adults that still lived there were either away working in San Luis or across the border picking lettuce or cotton.

A smile crossed a young Mexican boy's face as he saw the dust rising in the distance on the U.S. side. It was Waco and Joe. Nobody else drove down the road that fast. In fact, hardly anyone drove down that road.

He jumped on his small dirt bike and raced past the border guards who didn't look up from their card game and rode on a direct path toward the oncoming ambulance. Waco always stopped and picked him up. But this was Joe driving, and the Indian was always messing with him. The ambulance didn't slow down and the boy knew he was in trouble. He swerved out of the way at the last minute. He couldn't keep control of his bike and it shot off the road and fell into the ditch.

The ambulance sped past him, sped across the border without stopping. The entry into Mexico didn't phase the guards.

"Gin," the Mexican guard said, laying down his cards and smiling.

"Shit," the U.S. guard said. "You know, we really should check those kids? No telling what they're bringing across the border."

"You check them when they come out. There's nothing they could bring into Mexico that we ain't already got or that we don't need."

"Yeah, they're okay I guess. Here, it's your deal," the U.S. guard said as the Mexican boy raced back across the border.

"*Jesus*," he yelled. "*Que paso con* you, kid?"

The boy kept going without looking back until he finally caught up to the ambulance that had pulled up in front of Mama Lo's.

"Hey man, you coulda smashed my bike," he said, nursing a scraped arm as Joe stepped out of the ambulance.

"Sure we are, buddy. Just keeping you on your toes," Joe laughed. "How's your sister?"

"I ain't got no sister," Jesus said flatly.

"Come on, kid, help me unload the water."

Jesus jumped on the running board of the ambulance and looked inside.

"Hey, Waco. Where you going?"

"We're heading for Yuma if it's any of your business," Sarah said.

"Yuma?" *Jesus* said. "Can I come?"

"No, we got to take care of some business," Sarah

answered curtly.

"Let him come," Waco said from beneath his hat. "It don't make no difference."

"Come on, Jesus," Joe shouted, deliberately pronouncing the boy's name in English instead of *Haysus* in Spanish. "Give me a hand with these water bottles."

The inside of Mama's Lo's was like a museum dedicated to the Mexican Revolution, with memorabilia all over the adobe walls. A large portrait of Poncho Villa hung over the long wooden bar where Mama Lo stood. Dressed in a straight white Indian shift, the squat old woman had a round head, the broad nose of an Indian, with small almond shaped black eyes that were slightly crossed so they gave the impression she was never really looking at you. The brown eyes were buried between heavy slits of flesh which were the only evidence of the half Chinese blood that flowed through her veins.

"*Donde es mi* Waco? He suppose to bring water today," she said in broken English.

"Had an accident," Joe said, putting two water bottles down.

"Accident? *Què clasé*? What kind accident he have? He okay, *sí?*"

"Sure, sure, he's okay. But Grandma Poppy, she's dead," Joe said, arranging the water bottles in the corner of the cafe.

"*Dios mio*," Mama Lo said, making the sign of the cross. "*Pobre* Poppy. How is my Waco? Him okay?"

"Taking care of business Mama Lo. You know," the handsome Indian boy said, walking up to the bar. "Can't tell how he's taking it. Kinda quiet. You know Waco."

Mama Lo poured two glasses of tequila, offering one to Joe. She held her glass up. "To Poppy, may the good Virgin bless her. *Salud.*" She downed the clear cactus liquor in one gulp.

Joe looked at his glass. His stomach still hadn't settled from the T-bird he and Waco drank the night before, but he knew it would be impolite to refuse. He threw the tequila down his throat. It burned all the way, and then he fought back the salt water his stomach threw back at him.

Jesus lugged in the other bottles one at a time, dragging them across the floor.

"Guess Waco'll be going away now," Mama Lo said. "All the *gringos vamos* when they ain't got nothing to keep them here. We *indios*, we got nowhere else to go. This our home. *Gringos* can go anywhere. Only one hombre try to do something for us *indios*, Joe. Pancho," she said proudly, nodding her head around in the direction of the portrait of Pancho Villa above her. "Only my Pancho fought for us *indios*, but they killed him," she said.

"Listen Mama, we got to go." Joe didn't want to hear the stories again; about how the great Mexican revolutionary general had come to Mama Lo's cafe before he led his army against the corrupt Mexican government, and how she hid him from the U.S. Army that crossed the border to capture him.

"You bring Waco in," she insisted. "You boys got to

eat like always..."

"No Mama Lo. We got Grandma's body in the ambulance. Taking her to Yuma to get fixed up for burying. We don't get going she'll start to rot in this heat."

"Hey, Joe. Waco says let's go," *Jesus* said, dragging the last bottle across the floor.

"See you soon. Mama," Joe said.

"*Sí, sí,* you take good care of *Señora* Poppy. She no should start to smell," Mama said. "Tell Waco he have *familia* here. We all *familia, sí...*"

Joe hurried out the door. He slid a pair of aviation sunglasses over his broad nose to shield his eyes from the glaring desert morning sun. The air was sweet from the rain, but it would soon be dusty and thick from the heat that consumed everything in the desert.

He saw Maria, the sister *Jesus* said he didn't have, approaching the ambulance. Her long black hair flowed over a skimpy blouse, and she walked in small steps because of the tight skirt that confined her long brown legs. She smiled and nodded to him. He watched admiringly as she stepped onto the running board of the ambulance.

Waco allowed himself to smile at the sight of Maria's shining black eyes. Sarah looked away.

"Hi Waco. How come you didn't come last night?" Maria asked. "It was my day off. I expected you."

"I'm sorry. I had some trouble," Waco said.

"How's tricks, Maria?" Sarah said sarcastically.

"I missed you. I look forward to our talking together," the Mexican girl said, ignoring Sarah's remark.

"His grandmother died last night," Sarah said coldly.

"Is true, Waco?" Maria said, refusing to acknowledge the girl sitting next to him.

"She was very old," Waco said.

"*Lo siento mucho,*" Maria said, running her hand soothingly across his bare arm.

Joe stepped up to the truck. "Better get going. Jesus, get in the back," he said, using the English pronunciation again.

"Where you going. *hermanito*?" Maria shouted. "You no can go nowhere."

"I'm going to Yuma with my buddies," *Jesus* shouted back.

"Ay, that boy," Maria said, stepping off the ambulance. "You keep an eye on him, Waco. He never been to Yuma. Don't let the *Migra* catch him."

"He'll be all right," Waco said.

"You need anything, Waco, you remember, I'm your friend." She stepped back onto the running board and lightly kissed him on the cheek.

Joe started the engine as the back doors of the ambulance slammed shut. The gears ground and he released the heavy clutch. The ambulance jerked forward, and rolled back toward the border crossing.

"Jesus," Joe shouted back at the Mexican boy who was in a state of semi-shock after stumbling over the old woman's body. "What kind of name is that, Jesus? That's like naming someone God," he laughed.

"Don't step on Grandma," Waco said.

"You shouldn't talk to that girl," Sarah said. "It ain't right."

"Forget it, Sarah," Waco said. "She's a good kid. I don't care what she does."

* * *

"Gotya this time, you taco vendor," the U.S. guard laughed, proudly slamming his cards on the table just as the ambulance sped by. "Going down with five."

The Mexican guard smiled. "You think those kids got marijuana in their truck?"

"Huh, you think so?"

"*Quén sabe*...can't tell with kids these days, *gringo*. They get caught could be your job."

"Better call in. Have them stopped," the U.S. guard said, getting up to go into the small building on his side of the border.

The Mexican guard quickly changed some cards around.

"There, that will take care of those kids if they're trying to pull a fast one," the U.S. guard said, stepping from the building. "Now, where were we?"

"You went down with five. I hit you now on your kings and on your threes and go down with four. My game, *gringo*."

"The U.S. guard looked at the cards incredulously. "Shit...it's time for the morning movie. I'm going to watch TV."

Chapter Five

"Railroad's been through and gone...years ago,"
                                            -Luke

"I can't believe it. Poppy Merkins gone," Suzie said,
more to herself then to the other four old people sitting around the Pass Time. Suzie was the youngest of
the group, only sixty, except if you asked she'd tell you
she wasn't a year over fifty-five, She had refused to
give in to old age and boredom. Everyday she dressed
up in her finest, and never missed her weekly beauty
appointment in Yuma where the gray was dyed away,
replaced by bleach blonde and done up in a bouffant.
No one knew where she had come from, only that she
had arrived in town years earlier and taken rooms at
the Pass Time. Everyone knew she was Sheriff Merkins
mistress, everyone but Poppy Merkins, but no one
talked about it, and if truth be known, Poppy probably knew but didn't care. After the Sheriff died Suzie

stayed on, and became close friends with Poppy Merkins.

Sid stood quietly behind the bar as the news of Waco's grandmother's death sank into the remaining residents of Norte del Sur. He looked at his lifelong partner, Luke. For the first time he noticed that his friend had grown old; his six foot five was now bent over in a slight stoop, and what was once thick black hair had started to thin and turn white.

Luke handed a handkerchief to his wife, Mattie, whose tanned face was rutted with lines burnt in by the desert sun added maturity to her natural beauty. Her once blond hair had turned white which she carelessly folded into loose braids. She sat silently in front of the TV, tears running down her bony cheeks.

Bertha sat in the opposite chair, her eyes glued to the flickering images on the black and white screen. Suzie said Bertha's Indian blood allowed her to age well. Her face was unwrinkled, her skin bronze and her short hair was thick and black with handsome streaks of silver. But life had not been as kind to her mind; too many memories; too many hard times; too much abuse. Bertha had a tough time concentrating on anything but the TV for long, and her mind wandered randomly over the seventy years of her life.

"The Sheriff ain't going to be pleased," she said.

"What's that you said, Bertha?" Suzie asked.

"Sheriff Merkins. Won't be happy about it," Bertha muttered.

"Don't be silly, Bertha. Lemuel Merkin's been dead and gone for years," Luke said. "Dead and gone."

"Oh yes. Forgot. Wonder what's on the afternoon

movie," Bertha said, picking up the TV Guide from the wooden floor.

For a few minutes the only sound was from the characters of "*As The World Turns*" as they played out their daily tragedies.

"Guess we'll have to prepare a place for her," Mattie said, and then broke into sobs.

"Don't you worry about it," Sid said. "Me and Luke will take care of that."

"Where's my Sarah?" Mattie said suddenly, her sobs stopping as abruptly as they had begun.

"Went to town with the boys," Sid said.

"She's coming back? She hasn't left me?" Mattie said, her voice trembling.

"Don't worry, girl. They're all coming back. Tourist season. They'll be back," Sid said.

"Tourists?" Luke said. "I ain't holding my breath."

"This is the year," Sid said. "I feel it in my bones. You know what I mean. You get a feeling."

"I'm sorry," Mattie said. "I just couldn't take it if Sarah left me like her mother did."

Luke remained quiet. He had silently brooded since his daughter had left her baby girl with them and run off with that fast talking smart-ass from New Orleans. When he found out she had been killed in Louisiana he didn't have the heart to tell the others. He knew Mattie would fall apart if she knew.

"Now, now," Suzie said comfortingly. "As long as we're here..."

"Sure, that's the spirit," Sid said. "And this is the year. I can feel it in my bones."

"If something only happened around here," Luke

said. "Put this place back on the map. Trouble is, folks ain't interested in history these days. Gotta give them something exciting, like...like on TV."

"Railroad be coming through soon," Bertha said suddenly. "Everything be different when the railroad comes through."

They all looked at her.

"That was years ago, Bertha. Railroad's been through and gone...years ago," Luke said.

"Oh," Bertha said, and looked back into the TV Guide. "Bill Holden Western on at noon. Should be a good show."

Chapter Six

"Can't tell with kids these days.
-Sheriff Morrison

Tex walked into Daisy's Diner as though he controlled the life there the same way he held control over the highway. He eyed Daisy as she emerged from the kitchen. She liked the way his eyes seemed to undress her. She felt a nervous excitement at the sight of the six foot tall truck driver. Forty-two years old, abandoned by her husband, and stuck in the diner, Tex was the closest thing to affection and excitement she had. He made her feel attractive, and the fact was, she was a good looking woman. Her sumptuous body was hidden under a full dress, and she wore low cut blouses to show off her large bosom. She hid the emerging gray in her hair with dye, and covered the thin lines that had begun to appear around her mouth and eyes with pancake makeup. She knew in the back of her mind that she was probably just one of many woman Tex had between there and San Anton, but maybe someday he would take her away with him.

"Coffee?" she asked coyly, knowing full well what he was after.

"Put out the sign," he said.

"Can't do that. It's near lunch," she smiled.

"Put out the sign," he repeated, reaching across the counter and fondling her breast.

She playfully slapped his hand. "I'll lose too much money. I can't play with you today," she giggled.

Tex pulled a ten dollar bill out of his pocket and stuffed it into her blouse.

"Put out the sign."

Then he grabbed her under her arms and pulled her across the counter, kissing her hard on the lips. She resisted feebly for a minute, and then slid the rest of her body across the counter and into his lap.

"You said you'd bring me a present," she murmured.

"Next time, baby," he said, standing with her still clutched to him. He drug her over to the door of the diner, pressing his mouth next to hers, as if to keep her from talking, and turned the "open" sign around to "closed."

A dusty squad car pulled into the driveway of the diner. The driver, a slender man with a tan face etched with lines like a road map, noticed Tex's trailer truck and frowned to himself. His starched khaki uniform and badge identified him as a deputy sheriff.

"Have to go into Yuma for lunch, Sheriff," he said with a straight face to the man sitting next to him whose fat body was stuffed into a light tan suit. He wore a western tie was held together by a metal slid that read "Arizona" in brass. The color raised in the man's neck.

"What kinda of cow town shit is this, Hudnel! It's lunch time ain't it? This is a diner, ain't it! I'll see what the hell's going on."

Deputy Hank, as he was called, watched as the other man slammed out of the squad car and walked up to the diner. Hank didn't like the new sheriff. By all rights he should have taken over when Sheriff Garrett died under "mysterious circumstances" a month before. Matt Morrison was a political appointee by the Republican governor at the behest of the State Representative from Yuma County, and Hank was a Democrat. They told him he was too close to retirement anyway. But, besides that, Morrison didn't understand what being a sheriff in a border county meant. Gerrett had been the the son of the famous Pat Garrett who had gunned down Billy the Kid, and if there was anything Hank had learned from him in twenty years on the job, it was when to look the other way, who to leave alone, and that when in doubt it was federal jurisdiction. Didn't old man Garrett always say: 'If they are Mexicans, call Immigration; if it's drugs, call Drug Enforcement; if it's gambling, make sure they ain't cheating and get your cut; if it's prostitution, call me.'

Hank knew what was going on inside Daisy's, but he figured he'd let the new sheriff find out for himself.

* * *

Morrison banged on the diner door. "What's going on in there? Open up!" He banged on the door again. "It's Sheriff Morrison!" he yelled, as if the mere mention of his title was all it took to make things happen.

The door opened a crack. Tex stuck his naked torso out, looking down at the pudgy Sheriff.

"What the hell's wrong with you, boy. Can't you read? It says closed!"

"How come this diner isn't open?" Morrison said with as much authority as he could muster as he looked up at the giant truck driver. "Where is the proprietor?"

"The who?" Tex said.

"The owner. Where's the owner?"

Tex saw the Sheriff's hand move toward the holster that was concealed inside his blue blazer. "I must insist on seeing the owner."

"No need for that Sheriff. Daisy?" Tex called into the diner. "Man here wants to see you." He opened the door, exposing Daisy, sprawled out half undressed on one of the tables.

"Sorry Sheriff. I'm closed for lunch. Come back for dinner," she said.

Tex half shut the door. "Satisfied, Mr. Sheriff. Now, if you don't mind, I'm about to have lunch." He shut the door in Morrison's face and turned back to Daisy. "Shit, what an asshole."

Hank laughed to himself as he saw his boss stomping back to the squad car.

"Run a check on that truck, Hudnel," the Sheriff

said as he dropped into the passenger seat.

"Rodger, Sheriff," Hank said dutifully.

Just then the Sheriff's head turned toward the highway in time to catch the World War II ambulance speed by.

"Forget it, deputy. That vehicle matches the description we got from the Norte del Sur border guard…"

"But Sheriff. I thought you wanted me to run a check…"

"I want you to go after that vehicle!"

"What, that. That's just Joe…"

"Would you do like a tell you, deputy!" the Sheriff shouted, the red in his neck rising into his fat cheeks.

"Yes, sir," Hank said. He started the engine, banging his foot on the gas and skidding the car around in the dirt parking lot forcing the Sheriff to grab hold of the window so as not to slide across the seat. He flipped on the siren and red lights and took off down the highway after the ambulance, leaving a cloud of dust floating over Daisy's Diner.

The ambulance pulled over to the side of the highway in response to the squad car's siren. Hank stopped behind it and shut the siren off.

"Go investigate, deputy," Morrison ordered. "I'll cover you."

Hank watched incredulously as the new sheriff pulled a long barreled forty-five revolver from a holster hidden under his sports coat. He marveled as he didn't even know it was there because of Morrison's fat body.

"Get going, Hudnel. If there's a problem I'll open up."

"No need for that. Sheriff. I know these kids."

"How do you know? Can't tell with kids these days. Roust them!"

Hank walked up to the driver's side of the ambulance. "How's she going, Joe?"

"What's the hassle, deputy Hank?" Joe asked. "I wasn't speeding, was I?"

"Sorry kids. New Sheriff. Watched too many cop shows."

"Get those people out of the vehicle!" Morrison shouted, steadying his revolver on the open door of the squad car.

"Got a call to stop you from the border guard," Hank said apologetically.

"Cassidy reported us?" Waco said from under his hat. "What's gotten into him?"

"Have to ask you kids to step out of the car," Hank said.

Waco glanced back at Jesus who ducked down and slid next to the body of the dead woman. Hank caught a glimpse of the Mexican boy, but pretended he didn't notice.

"Draw your gun," Waco said. "We'll make it look good for the new sheriff."

"Ah, come on. That ain't necessary," Hank said.

"Come on deputy Hank," Sarah added. "If we're going to be stopped, let's do it like in the movies."

"All right, all right," Hank said, and reluctantly drew his revolver from its holster.

"Say something cool. Hank." Joe said.

"Like what?" the deputy said, feeling foolish

"Come on, man. You watch TV," Waco egged him on.

"Okay you kids," Hank said loud enough for Morrison to hear. "Get your asses outta that ambulance with your hands up."

"That's pretty good, Deputy Hank," Joe said, slowly opening the door, and adding loudly, "Don't shoot, deputy. We're coming out."

The teenagers slid out of the driver's side of the ambulance; Joe, then Sarah, and finally Waco.

"This new guy, he's a real asshole ain't he," Waco whispered to Hank as he raised his hands into the air.

"Should've been my job," Hank said.

Morrison cautiously approached the ambulance with his gun held at the ready. "Good work, deputy."

"We ain't done nothing. Mr. Sheriff, sir," Waco said sarcastically. "Just going to Yuma to see an undertaker."

"Don't sass me, boy," Morrison snapped. "Just keep your hands up." He looked at Joe suspiciously. "You're an Injun, ain't you?"

"Chiricahua." Joe answered. "Me no like white eyes."

"Don't get smart, Injun. We gotta report you kids may be smuggling controlled substance into the U.S. Open the back, deputy."

"You don't want to do that," Waco said.

"Shut up, kid. I said open it up, deputy. I'll keep them covered."

Hank stepped to the back of the ambulance and hesitated. He'd known the kids for years. They weren't smuggling anything. But he also knew Jesus was in the back. If Morrison found him, he'd surely insist on turning the kid over to the Immigrations.

"Open it, deputy!" Morrison demanded. "It ain't hard to see these juveniles are hiding something."

Hank slowly opened the rear doors of the World War II ambulance. For a moment he was struck dumb as he stared into the dead eyes of Poppy Merkins staring coldly back at him.

"Well, deputy. What's back there!" Morrison shouted. "You see anything?"

"It's my grandmother," Waco offered. "She died last night."

"What the hell," Morrison said. "Hank, cover these people. I'll investigate myself." He walked to the back of the ambulance without waiting for Hank to take his place. He glanced into the back of the ambulance, all the time holding his gun on the three teenagers. "I'll be damned. Looks like a homicide," he said.

"Don't think so," Hank said. "That there's Poppy Merkin's, Waco's grandmother, like he said."

Waco started to approach the rear of the ambulance. "We're taking her into Yuma to get her fixed up for burying," he said.

"Just you hold it right there," Morrison shouted. "Didn't nobody give you permission to move."

Waco stopped and lifted his hands back in the air.

Hank saw Jesus' foot sticking out from the tarp next to the body. He quickly closed the back doors. "Sure, that's Poppy, alright. Guess you'll be burying her next to Sheriff Merkins, eh Waco," he said.

"Lemuel Merkins?" Morrison said. "*The* Sheriff Lemuel Merkins?"

"One and the same," Hank said, wiping the sweat that had begun pouring down his neck. This here's Lemuel Merkin's widow."

"Why hell, we read about Sheriff Merkins in Arizona history. He's a legend."

"You see, Sheriff," Hank said, slowly closing the doors to the ambulance. "These kids is all right."

"Not so fast, deputy," Morrison said, relaxing his gun hold on the teenagers. "There's got to be some law against transporting a dead body without a proper health permit. How come you kids didn't report this to the authorities?"

"Had to get her to Yuma before her body gets ripe, Sheriff," Joe offered.

Morrison rolled the answer around in his mind for a minute. The late morning sun was beating down hard now and swarms of flies were beginning to buzz around the truck. He looked up at a group of buzzards circling overhead. He finally came to a decision.

"Better get that body on ice somewhere before it becomes a health problem." he sighed, putting his revolver back into its custom leather holster under his blue blazer. "Come on, deputy. Let's get some lunch." He returned to the squad car and got in.

Hank walked over to Waco, and spoke in a hushed tone. "Sorry about your grandmother, Waco. And keep that Mexican kid out of sight, would you."

"Sure thing, deputy Hank," Waco said.

"She was a helluva gal, your grandmother was..."

Waco watched as the lanky deputy walked back to the squad car. Waco had never noticed before, but Hank with the bow legs of a cowboy. How'd he ever get bowed legs from riding in a squad car Waco wondered.

Chapter Seven

Coffins and ice cream

The only thing Jesus saw was the bright red bow tie. Everything else about the skinny man standing in front of the Final Sunset Mortuary was black and white; the face, the hair, the suit, the bony hands that stuck out from the cardboard starched shirt cuffs.

Could there be this many buildings in the whole world? He had looked out the back window of the ambulance as they rolled into Yuma, his eyes wide. In all his nine years he had never been outside his little village on the border. He had seen it on TV, but he never believed the Golden Arches really existed; Burger Kings, Taco Bells everywhere. And buildings; bigger than the hills around the village. Sure, everyone had told him it was just like on TV, but he never really believed it. Once his sister wanted to take him to San Luis with her, but he refused. He knew what Maria did in San Luis. He had asked Waco to take him to Yuma with him, but Waco kept saying the *Migra* would catch him and put him in jail.

The man with the red bow tie looked over the papers Waco had handed him. He lifted his pale eyes from them and said in a high voice, "If you will leave the deceased with us, we will have her ready for burial in two hours. Shall we deliver? There will be an extra charge if you want her delivered. We don't go to..." He looked back at the paper. "...Norte del Sur."

"We'll be back for her in a couple of hours," Waco said.

Sarah whispered something into Waco's ear.

"Don't we get to pick a casket?" Waco asked.

"Pick a casket?" The man in the bow tie looked indignant. "There's no instructions to that effect in this contract."

"That contract's forty years old," Sarah said. "Mrs. Merkin's been paying you people five dollars a month for forty years. We should at least be able to pick out a casket."

"That's $2,400," Joe said. "That should buy the best box in the house"

"This agreement is so old, I do nothing but lose money," the man said, walking toward the back of the ambulance. "The deceased is in here, I take it."

"You'd better take her quick. Mister," Jesus said, seeing his chance to add his voice, although he didn't know what was going on. "*Señora* Merkins, she starting to smell bad, man."

"Shut up, Jesus," Sarah said, pushing the boy out of the way.

"Hey man, this is bullshit," Joe said. "Let's take her back and the chief will bury her in the Chiricahua way. No fuss, no muss."

"No," Waco said. "She paid for this. She wants to be buried in a casket next to Grandpa Lemuel."

"Okay, but you white people sure have strange ways," the Indian said, and opened the back of the ambulance.

The man in the red bow tie took a white handkerchief from his breast pocket, covered his mouth and nose and peeked through the open doors. "Got her here in the nick of time," he said, and then shouted into the open doors of the Final Sunset Mortuary. Two young Mexican men came out. They were dressed in white frock coats. As soon as they hit the sunlight the heavy grease in their slicked back black hair started to melt, and it dripped down their brown faces like candle wax. "Bring the gurney over here and get the deceased inside."

Jesus watched as the two assistants unceremoniously pulled the body from the back of the ambulance and dropped Poppy Merkins onto the gurney.

"Hey, you guys left Mexico to do this?" Jesus said.

"Get outta the way, *cabron.* " one of the two assistants said.

Poppy Merkins's eyes seemed to stare at him. "How come they didn't close her eyes," Jesus muttered. "They should have closed her eyes"

* * *

No one spoke as the ambulance slowly made its way through the streets of Yuma. A wind had blown in off the desert, bringing with its hot blasts rolling tumble weeds and sheets of sand which left a white film over the asphalt streets as nature sought to reclaim that which had been taken from her.

"They should have let you pick a casket," Sarah finally broke the silence.

"That's a lot of money, $2,400," Joe said.

"Forget it." Waco's voice drifted from underneath his hat.

A blast of hot air blew against the side of the ambulance. Joe tightened his grip on the wheel and shifted down to second as dust coated the windshield.

"But they ripped you off, Waco. They plain robbed you," Sarah protested.

"We ought to go in there and take the best casket they got," Jesus said, sticking his head between Waco and Sarah from the rear of the ambulance. "That's what Pancho Villa would do,"

"Shut up," Waco and Sarah said in unison.

"That's what Mama Lo says." The boy slipped back out of sight.

"Let me off here," Waco said.

Joe put his foot on the brake and pulled over to the curb.

"I'll meet you guys back at the mortuary in two hours." Waco opened the door. The hot air blew into the ambulance.

"Where are you going?" Sarah asked.

"Never mind. I got some business to take care of," he said, and slammed the door closed.

Sarah started to roll down her window, but Joe put his hand on her shoulder. "Leave him alone, Sarah. I think he's going to see his mother."

"Hey, what are we going to do now?" Jesus said, sticking his head back over the front seat. "We going to MacDonald's or something?"

"You better be cool, kid, or we'll turn you over to the *Migra*," Joe said.

"I have to go to the market," Sarah said. "Got to pick some things up for Uncle Sid."

"There you go, Jesus,"—Joe still used the English pronunciation— "We're going to show you a genuine supermarket." He jammed the gear into first, and the ambulance jerked forward.

Sarah opened the window and looked behind, hoping to catch a glimpse of Waco. But he had already disappeared into the clouds of blowing sand and dust that blanketed the desert city.

The Mexican boy had never seen so much food all in one place at one time. He wandered down the aisles of the Desert Horn of Plenty Supermarket dumping items into a shopping basket as Joe and Sarah casually followed behind him.

"Mama Lo will want some of this, and I think we can use this..." Jesus said joyfully as he filled the shopping cart.

Sarah had loaded ten commercial sized cans of red kidney beans into her own cart, along with ten bottles of Bromo Seltzer.

Joe finally caught up with Jesus. "How much money you have?" he asked.

Jesus looked up at him and then dug into his pocket and pulled out a handful of coins. There were five pesos, three dimes, four nickels and twenty centavos.

"I don't think that's going to do it, kid," he said. "You'd better put it all back."

"Ah, man. We could use this stuff."

"If you can't pay you can't play," Joe said.

Jesus looked hurt. "Pancho Villa would have just taken it," he muttered.

The boy caught up with Sarah and Joe at the check stand. He took a Three Musketeers candy bar from a rack and got in line behind a fat woman.

"Excuse me, *señora*," he said. I'm with them."

The woman looked at the boy and then at Joe and Sarah. "You'll just have to wait your turn," she said in a tone that let Jesus know he'd better do as he was told.

When the woman got to the check stand she stared at Sarah and Joe for a moment, and then commented to the checker, just loud enough for everyone to hear; "It was that damn Martin Luther King, you know. Now look, that white girl with a...Mexican."

The checker just smiled politely.

"He ain't no Mexican, lady. He's an Indian..." Jesus piped in .

The woman ignored him.

"I'm Mexican. He's an Indian," Jesus insisted. But no one paid any attention.

Sarah and Joe started walking to the door of the

market as the checker bagged the woman's groceries.

"How much?" Jesus asked, holding out the Three Musketeers in one hand, and his pocketful of change in the other.

The checker finished with the woman who looked down at the boy disapprovingly. "Where did you get that Mexican money?" she demanded. "Why, I'll bet this boy's in this country illegally," she added, aiming her remark at the checker who tried to ignore her.

"That will be thirty-five cents," he told Jesus, and rang up the purchase as the boy fished through the coins for the right change.

Suddenly a siren sounded and all the lights in the store began going on and off.

"Damn, it's the *Migra*!" Joe said to Sarah. "They must have caught Jesus."

"Let's get him and get out of here," Sarah said.

Jesus was looking for an escape route, but the fat woman blocked his exit. There was no where to go.

Just as Sarah and Joe got back to the check stand, a large red cheeked man in a white shirt and tie was standing there. "You've done it! You've really done it!" he said to the fat woman.

"No, no," the checker said. "It's the boy."

"I didn't do nothing," Jesus protested.

"Well, I'll be," the man in the white shirt said, pushing the fat woman out of the way.

"We can explain everything." Joe said, trying to push his way past the woman who refused to budge.

"I don't believe this," she said. "I've been coming here for ten years and I've never been a Red Star winner."

"Red star what?" Joe said.

"Eh man. I didn't do nothing," Jesus said looking up at the big man who had a name tag designating him the General Manager.

"Nothing you say. What's this?" He grabbed the cash register receipt from the checker and held it up, just as a woman in a white blouse and tight skirt snapped a picture. "The Desert Horn of Plenty congratulates you son. You're our Red Star winner."

"Ten years." the fat woman moaned, "And this wetback kid wins for buying a candy bar."

Jesus looked around not knowing what was going on. "Winner? What's that?"

"Yes!" the man in the tie proclaimed. "You have just won twenty gallons of the world famous Desert Blossom ice cream in twenty-nine flavors. Our Red Star Winner!"

"You going to put my picture in the newspaper?" Jesus said.

The fat woman was still mumbling to herself as she loaded her groceries into her station wagon. Jesus came up behind her with three gallons of ice cream.

"This is for you lady. I hope you like butter pecan."

She looked at the boy, trying to decide whether she should smile. Finally she took the ice cream from him. "Well, it's the least you could do. I have spent thousands at this store, and I never got the Red Star," and a smile crept into her face as she took the ice cream from the boy.

* * *

"We're going to have to throw that stuff out. It's going to melt all over the back of my truck," Joe said. "Besides, we'll have to put Poppy Merkins back there. It wouldn't be right to get melted ice cream all over her."

Jesus was sitting in the back stuffing as much of the melting twenty-nine flavors into his mouth as he could. "Eh man. I ain't never won nothing before."

"Dump it, Jesus," Sarah said.

They pulled up in front of the Final Sunset Mortuary. Waco was standing by the door waiting for them. The man in the red bow tie came out from the office.

"Pull that thing around the rear," he instructed.

"You got a garbage can back there?" Joe yelled out the of window of the ambulance.

Waco and Sarah followed the mortician into the mortuary. They were lead to the back room. Waco looked into the plain pine box sitting on a gurney. Poppy Merkins stared back at him, her face draped in white satin material and painted in clownish makeup.

"Close it up," he said flatly.

"Wait a minute, Waco," Sarah said. She turned to the man in the red bow tie. "Is this the best you could do...a pine box!"

"It's what you get. What did you expect for five bucks a month."

"Come on, Sarah. Let's get out of her," Waco said.

Sarah followed behind him as he headed for the rear door. The two Mexican helpers in their white coats wheeled the coffin behind them.

"I don't believe this," Sarah said. "She paid out twenty-four hundred bucks, and all he can come up with is a pine box."

Joe and Jesus had just finished tossing what was left of the ice cream into a dumpster as the funeral parade came out of the mortuary.

"Better get her into the ground fast man," one of the Mexicans said. "The boss did a rush job."

Jesus licked the last of the ice cream from his fingers, and jumped in behind the pine coffin. Joe slammed the rear doors shut.

Chapter Eight

"I ain't going to forget you injun. This ain't over."
-Butch Boyle

No one spoke of Waco's absence at the burial. Whatever thoughts they had they kept to themselves; all but Mama Lo who kept saying, "Waco should be here. It no is right Waco isn't here."

There was no priest. The closest church was ten miles away on the reservation; a small Catholic mission. But Poppy Merkins wasn't Catholic anyway. A hot wind blew across the small cemetery of Norte del Sur. The plain pine box sat by an open hole next to another grave with a worn marble stone. Weeds had grown around it. The lettering was barely visible:

Lemuel Merkins
He shot the bad guys
and died a natural death
1875-1951

Sarah and Joe stood on one side. Mama Lo was at the foot of the grave. Sid stood at the head of the freshly dug hole, and the other older people stood on the other side. They were all dressed in their Sunday best; all but Bertha who hadn't accepted Poppy being dead, and refused to miss the afternoon movie to walk to the graveyard. They stood silently; the older ones thinking how they would soon follow Poppy Merkins into the arid dirt of the Arizona desert. The younger ones were there because it was the thing they were suppose to do. It was respect and pity; respect because Poppy Merkins was part of their lives—part of what gave meaning to their own existence: pity because her life had had its glory and had ended with none.

"There's no marker." Mattie said as tears streamed down her face.

"She's right," Suzie said. "It ain't right to bury a body with no marker."

"Don't worry," Sid said. "I made one. It's only wood, but we can't afford nothing else."

"Someone should say something," Luke said suddenly. "It's only fitting someone should say something." He looked at Sid.

"Me? I don't know no words. I mean, I know some, but I can't do it. You know what I mean." Sid stammered.

"Waco should be here," Mama Lo said.

"You should say something, Sid," Suzie said, putting her arm around Mattie who hadn't stopped crying since they had brought Poppy Merkins back from the funeral parlor.

"I dug the grave and made a marker," Sid said. "Ain't that enough. Hell, I ain't no preacher."

Just then they heard the sound of a drum, beating out a slow steady rhythm, and behind the drum a low chanting voice: "Ah ya, ah ya, ah ya."

Everyone looked up. It was the Old Chief in full paint and headdress, beating a drum and slowly dancing into the group. He circled them, beating the drum and chanting the burial song to his ancestors.

Joe looked over at Sarah. They picked up the ropes that harnessed the pine coffin. Sid and Luke picked up the other side, and they slowly lowered Poppy Merkins into the hole. The Old Chief kept beating the drum and chanting.

Mattie whispered, "it's just like Norte del Sur. We're slowly sinking into our graves. Soon it will all be gone," and she started sobbing again, staining Suzie's satin dress with her tears. The coffin made a dull thump as it hit the bottom of the pit. They slid the ropes out from under it. Luke, who had now appointed himself the expert on funerals, took up a handful of dirt and dropped it into the grave.

"It's how you do it," he said.

Sid glared at him for a second and then followed Joe and Sarah who had already tossed some dirt into the hole.

"Go ahead, girls," Luke said to the old women. The Old Chief stopped beating the drum for a moment and looked at this curious ritual. He shrugged and went back to beating the small drum and chanting.

Sid set up a wooden post with the words:

Poppy Merkins
Devoted Wife. '

Just then Jesus came running up. "They're tearing up the place," he shouted in excitement. He was nursing a bloody nose.

"*Cáyate niño!*" Mama Lo said. "What's the matter you. Have respect for the dead."

"But, they're tearing up the place," Jesus insisted.

"What...what are you doing boy? You're suppose to be watching the Pass Time," Sid said, stepping over the hole to reach the boy. "Who's doing what?"

"A bunch of rich boys. They're tearing up the place," Jesus said, out of breath. "I tried to stop them, but there was too many...they got my sister ..."

"Luke, Joe, let's go." Sid shouted.

"But, we ain't finished here," Luke said. "It ain't how its done."

"Never mind. Poppy will wait," Sid said. "You girls stay here."

Joe picked up the shovel and followed Sid, with Sarah right behind him.

"It ain't how it's done," Luke said again, and reluctantly hurried after the others.

"*Madre mia*, Waco should be here," Mama Lo said.

The Old Chief continued beating the drum and chanting as if in a trance.

* * *

They reached the hill that overlooked Norte Del Sur. The front of the Pass Time looked like a show room for Honda, Suzuki and Yamaha dirt bikes and dune buggies. About a dozen crew cut boys with Arizona U sweat shirts were milling around the entrance of the building, guzzling down bottles of Coors beer and tossing the empties onto the ground.

"We've been invaded," Luke said under his breath.

Suddenly they saw Maria run from the Pass Time into the street. Her blouse was torn in front, and she was barefoot. A muscular boy with short blonde hair and a cut-off sweat shirt came after her.

Her voice drifted up to the group on the hill. "Get away from me *cabrone*. Leave me alone..."

She fell to the ground as the other boys stood around her laughing and hooting.

Joe felt his blood rise. He found himself running wildly down the hill, whooping and shouting and waving the shovel as if it were a war lance.

The boys in front of the Pass Time stopped to look at the crazy man charging down the hill toward them.

"The kid's gone crazy," Sid said.

Sarah started down the hill after Joe. "Come on. We can't let him go down there alone," she called back at them.

Sid looked at Luke. "Guess we can't let the kid get killed," he said, and they followed in Sarah's dust down the low hill.

The blond crew cut, who the others called Butch, stood over Maria as Joe charged him.

Butch was not expecting a head on assault by the raging Indian waving a shovel. Had he been smart he would have moved, but instead he held his ground, believing the Indian would stop and confront him. He was wrong. Joe jumped over the girl and body slammed him to the ground. The boys around him stood with their mouths wide open, as shocked as he was. But Butch was a college wrestler and quickly regained his senses. He grabbed hold of the shovel handle and threw his attacker over.

Joe jumped to his feet and slammed the shovel into the college boy's surprised face, sending him reeling backward.

"Keep back," Joe warned the others, holding the shovel in front of him like a war lance.

Butch shook his head. Blood gushed from his nose. "Get the son-of-a-bitch," he screamed.

One of the boys grabbed Maria from behind. "Hey Injun," he shouted. "You want your Mex whore, come get her..." but he was stopped short as Maria slammed her knee into his groin, buckling the boy over. Sarah came up and kicked the boy in the behind, sending him sprawling onto the ground moaning in pain.

Two huge boys jumped in and held Joe. Several others took hold of the two girls. Butch came up and was punching Joe in the stomach as Luke and Sid ran up, huffing and puffing.

"What's going on here!" Sid demanded, as Luke stood behind him.

"Stay out of this old man," Butch shouted.

"This is my place," Sid said. "What's the matter with you kids?"

A smile crossed the college boy's face. "Your place! Is this anyway to treat customers? All we wanted was some beer and a little action. Hell, that's what border towns are for, aren't they." He walked over to Maria and toyed with her torn blouse. "Why else you got whores around here," he said.

"Leave her alone white boy," Joe moaned in pain.

"Take your hands off her you scum," Sarah said. "Who do you think you are?"

"Well, listen to the little cowgirl. Who am I?" Butch said, and walked over to one of the dune buggies and pulled out a twelve gauge shotgun. "I'm the boss," he shouted and shot at one of the Pass Time's windows which exploded from the blast. "That's who I am!"

Suddenly another shot rang out. A bullet kicked the dirt up in front of Butch. Everyone turned around. There they saw the Old Chief, standing by the touring car and holding a smoking Winchester rifle.

"The next one won't be low, white eyes," he said.

Sid walked up to the two boys that were holding Joe. "Let him go," he said.

Luke took the two girls from the other boys. Maria ran over and helped Joe as Sid took the shotgun from Butch.

"You boys better get. The Chief's been known to scalp young white boys," Sid said.

Butch wiped the blood from his nose, and walked over to Joe. "I ain't going to forget you injun. This ain't over."

"I look forward to it, white boy," Joe managed, as Maria held him up .

The boys got onto their Japanese machines and

roared out of town .

Maria and Sarah helped Joe into the Pass Time. Sid and Luke followed behind. As they entered they fell silent. The place had been trashed, and "ohhh, they broke the TV," Bertha moaned over and over again. "Why'd they have to break the TV."

Chapter Nine

"You going to kill somebody,"
-Old Mexican

Waco sat cross legged in the small hut, closely watching the old Mexican man who was inspecting his grandfather's revolver. He had known the old man since having stumbled across his shack in the desert several years before while he was wondering through the desert on the old pinto. He always wandered off into the desert alone when he needed to be alone and think.

Nacho had long black hair and a full beard streaked with gray. He told Waco he had been living there for over twenty years. There was nothing for him in Mexico, he said. Not since his leader Pancho Villa had been assassinated by his arch rival President Obregon in 1923. "They betrayed our revolution," he had told Waco. "The people looked to Pancho to make things right, but they killed him."

The night wind blew through the cracks in the boards, filling the room with hot dry air and a low whistling noise. Somewhere in the distance a coyote wailed at the full moon that had risen in the east.

"Well. Can it work?" Waco asked.

The old Mexican looked over the revolver like a doctor examining a patient with his dark eyes that twinkled under brown wrinkled eyelids.

"Is like the one I carried when I rode with General Villa. She's a good gun."

Waco had brought Grandpa Lemuel's six shooter to the old hermit. He didn't want to ask Luke or Sid if it worked. They would probably have taken it from him for their collection of historic artifacts that they kept on display in the Pass Time, although no one had taken an interest in it for years.

"Will it work?" Waco repeated.

"I was just a young kid then," the old man said. "A young macho kid full of ideas of glory and justice. Pancho, he was our leader. The *gringos* called him a *bandido*, you know."

"Yes, I know all about it," Waco said impatiently. "Mama Lo has told me a thousand times."

A look of nostalgia fell across the old man's face. "Ah yes, Mama Lo," he repeated with a sigh. "She was the most beautiful of women..."

"The gun," Waco said.

"Do you have a woman?" the old man asked.

"Well, there is someone, maybe....look, I didn't come here to talk about women," Waco said impatiently, not wanting to talk about the new feelings he was starting to have for Sarah. It confused him because they were more than brotherly, and he felt guilty thinking about it.

"The gun. Will it work?" Waco insisted.

The old man looked up and smiled. He stuck a cartridge into the revolver, pointed it at the wall, cocked the pistol and released the hammer. The small hut reverberated with the explosion, filling it with sweet smelling smoke. When the air cleared Waco saw a neat hole in the side of the hut where the bullet had passed through into the night.

"She work fine," the old man said. "Now, what you going to do with it? You going to kill somebody," he suddenly laughed out loud, exposing a mouth full of gold teeth.

"I'm going to do what needs doing," Waco said simply, remembering he had heard that line in a John Wayne movie. It sounded good to say it.

The old Mexican smiled. "I'll clean her up for you. She'll be good as new."

Waco pulled a bottle of tequila from his knapsack. "*Gracias viejo.*"

"*Bueno.* We drink and I tell you about Mexico and our Revolution."

"Well, did you bring it?" Daisy's voice floated from the kitchen of the diner to the counter where Tex had just sat down.

"What?" he shouted back. "Is that the way you greet your favorite customer?"

Daisy stuck her head out from the opening that separated the kitchen from the counter. "You promised you'd bring me something special this trip."

"Ain't I special enough," he laughed, and went behind the counter. "Look baby, I only got an hour. What do you say?" He reached through the opening and slid his hand into her loose fitting blouse. She didn't resist, but refused to smile. "I'll remember next time."

"You promise," She smiled coyly.

"Sure baby, I promise."

"Okay, I'll forgive you this one time. Come on."

Tex moved toward the swinging doors to the kitchen, unbuttoning his shirt as he went.

"Better put up the closed sign," Daisy said.

"Sure thing, baby."

Just as he got to the door he ran into Deputy Hank.

"Sorry pal, we're closed for an hour," Tex winked.

"Damnit Tex, where's a man suppose to eat?"

"I don't know about you, Hank, but I'm about to eat as soon as you leave."

"Someday that girl's going get on to you, Tex."

"I wouldn't lose no sleep over it," the half undressed truck driver said, easing the deputy sheriff out of the door.

"Say Tex. Whose driving your rig, anyway?" Hank said.

"No one. Its parked outside."

"Not no more. I just passed it going down the highway. Doing maybe eighty. I thought it was…"

Tex had already pushed past the deputy into the sun baked parking lot. His Mack truck and twenty five head of beef were gone.

"Goddamn Arizona!" he shouted.

Hank smiled to himself. I'll call it in if you like."

"You're not going after it?" Tex said, looking down the highway.

"Well, if you like, we can go look for it. But I wouldn't guarantee anything."

"Let me get my shirt," Tex said running back to the diner.

"Sure thing, Tex," Hank said, thoroughly enjoying himself.

When Tex emerged from the diner, Hank saw Daisy appear at the door holding her unbuttoned blose closed.

"You coming back honey?"

Tex ignored her and jumped into Hanks car. Hank tipped his hat to her.

"Howdy Daisy. Your looking mighty pretty today."

"Come on deputy. Let's get going," Tex shouted from the car.

Chapter Ten

"I got to do something or I'll die,"

-Waco

No one in Norte del Sur gave much thought to it when Deputy Hank stopped by and told them about Tex's cattle truck being stolen. In fact, most of them silently felt a measure of satisfaction in the heist by some unknown cattle thief. Sid suggested it might be the Floyd Gang come down from the north of the state as they were known to do. Hank agreed, saying he told the new sheriff the same thing.

The old folks didn't even suspect when the van pulled up a day later with a brand new marble tombstone with the engraving:

SHERIFF LEMUEL MERKINS
HE SHOT THE BAD GUYS
AND DIED A NATURAL DEATH
1875-1951

POPPY MERKINS
DEVOTED WIFE
SHE STOOD BY HER MAN
1898-1973

Sid insisted that it came from Poppy's daughter, but Mattie was convinced that Myrtle Merkins was probably drunk in some cheap motel in Yuma, and wouldn't have the money for a tomb stone anyway. "Has to be from some historical society or something like that," she argued.

Sarah thought differently, although she didn't let on. She had been worried because Waco hadn't been back for several days, ever since he failed to show up for the funeral. She hadn't put the highjacking of the cattle truck and the arrival of the tombstone together until she noticed the engraving under Poppy Merkin's name. It had to be written by Waco, it was one of Poppy's favorite songs, and wouldn't any historical society have known that. But the only way Waco could get enough money for a stone like that was to steal it.

Joe had also been worried about his friend Waco. He went across the border in search of him, knowing Waco often went to see Maria to talk when he was troubled.

Mama Lo said, "I told you. When the white people get a chance they go. Only us *indios* stay," and then she went on about Pancho Villa and stories he had heard a thousand times about the Mexican Revolution. He walked out somewhere around where she insisted General Pershing was sent across the border to hunt the Mexican revolutionary down after he had attacked the town of Arizona even though everyone told her it had been in Columbus, New Mexico.

Joe walked down the dirt street to an adobe cottage where Maria stayed with her brother. It was still morning, so he figured he'd find her there, perhaps still asleep from a long night's work in San Luis.

The door was open and so he stepped in out of the dusty heat. He had never been in her house. He was surprised to see that the interior of the modest cottage was well furnished with a new couch, end tables, plush carpeting and a small TV. Cool air blew down from a swamp cooler on the roof.

"If you're looking for Jesus, he's out somewhere." Maria stood in the doorway that led to the bedroom where he caught a glimpse of a brass bed. He had never seen her without makeup. She wore a short hip-hugging white slip, and her long black hair draped over her brown shoulders. A small gold cross hung neatly between her high breasts.

"I'm...I'm looking for Waco," he stammered, suddenly embarrassed.

"Joe, you okay? You look sick."

He caught his breath. "Yeah. You seen Waco?".

"What you mean, you're looking for Waco? He no is in Norte del Sur?"

"We haven't seen him in a couple of days. I thought he might be here," Joe said, unable to take his eyes off her.

Maria suddenly felt shy under the young Indian's gaze. Her reaction surprised her. He had always acted indifferent to her. He never knew that she secretly liked him, but after he had come to her rescue at the Pass Time she had hoped he had finally noticed her. Adn now that it seemed he was interested she felt like a innocent teenager. She grabbed her bathrobe and pulled it tightly around her.

"Why you think he would come to me?" she asked.

"Well, I always thought that you and he...that is, I..."

"Me and Waco, we are like brother and sister. We like to talk together, that is all."

Joe smiled for a moment, and then turned back to the door. "I'm sorry I bothered you."

"No Joe. Don't go. Stay and talk to me for a minute." "Tell me what has happened to my Waco. I'll get you a beer, okay?"

"Well, for a minute." Joe said, not really wanting to leave, but frightened by his sudden attraction to this girl whom he had never allowed himself to think of as anything more than another poor Mexican girl forced to do what she had to do in order to support herself and her family.

She brought a frosty bottle of Mexicali from the small kitchen and handed it to him. "I think maybe

Waco, he went into the desert. Many times when he is unhappy he just get on that old horse of his and rides," she said, sitting on the couch.

Joe continued to stand by the door.

She didn't want himto get away now that she knew he was attracted to her. "Come, sit down," she insisted, patting the couch with her hand. "You aren't afraid of me are you?" she smiled.

He felt his face get hot. He had never been afraid of anything, but he was suddenly terrified by the feelings the young woman aroused in him.

"We think he..he might be in some trouble."

"Hombre. I never see you so...so speechless. Joe, I think you are a little scared by me," she smiled.

"I better get going."

Maria stood up and came over to him as he lingered in the doorway. She brushed his hand with hers. Joe felt the warmth of her body radiate through him.

"You no worry about Waco. He can take care of himself. You find him, and then come back. Maybe we can talk."

"Yeah, sure," Joe said, and he gulped down the beer and handed her the empty bottle.

"You guys come here if you need to. No matter what the reason, you come here. If I see Waco I'll send Jesus to find you."

He walked back out into the blaring sunlight and found that he was soaking in sweat. He looked at his hands. They were shaking. Part of him wanted to rush back into the cottage and take Maria into his arms. But instead he hopped into the ambulance and headed back across the border.

"That was not cool," he muttered to himself, and turned up the radio. Johnny Cash and June Carter signing a love song. He quickly switched the radio off.

The full moon cast a blue hue off the shiny marble surface of the new tombstone. A lone figure stood in front of the fresh grave. His Double eagle cowboy boots dug into the ground. He had been standing there about fifteen minutes not knowing that a pair of loving eyes were patiently watching.

Finally a voice whispered, "Waco."

He turned and saw Sarah, standing behind the lone Oak tree that had managed to survive the Arizona wasteland, as if nourished by the dead that were buried there in the small Norte del Sur graveyard.

"Waco, we've been worried about you."

"It looks good, doesn't it," he said.

Sarah came over to him and looked down at the tombstone, and then at the revolver in Waco's belt. She unconsciously took hold of his hand. "It was you, wasn't it," she said. "You stole Tex's truck and used the money to buy the stone."

"Oh, Tex's precious truck. Yeah, it was me. But I only sold the cattle. They'll find his truck okay. 'Sides, I only got hold of two of them steers. The others ran off into the desert."

She let go of his hand and folded her arms in front of her. "Waco. What's wrong with you? You could get into a lot of trouble doing something like that."

Waco looked back at the gravestone. Then he looked at Sarah, how pretty she was, and he felt a stirring in the pit of his stomach.

"It ain't right," he said. "It ain't right them not having a proper marker. When things ain't right, you got to do something, even if it means taking chances..."

"Even if it means breaking the law?"

"Laws don't make things right, Sarah."

They stood there quietly for a minute listening to the silence of the desert. Somewhere a dog was howling at the moon.

"How are the old folks?" Waco asked. "They didn't take it too hard? I wanted to be at the funeral, only..."

"Well, for your information, while you were out rustling cattle, a bunch of college kids came into town on their dirt bikes. They were drinking beer and smashed up the Pass Time. Busted the TV and beat up Joe. Attacked Maria and would have...if it wasn't for Joe."

"The TV! Damn Sarah, what's the folks going to do without a TV. See, I told you things ain't right. And what was Maria doing there?"

Sarah was surprised. She had thought his first reaction would have been concern for Maria, not the old folks and their smashed TV.

"She said she came to keep an eye on Jesus. She was worried the *migra* would pick him up. They were watching the place while everyone was up at the graveyard."

"What did Deputy Hank say?"

"Said nothing. One of them boys was Rowdy Boil's kid. He's some big wig in Yuma or something."

"Yeah, I know who that is," Waco said.

"Said the Sheriff wouldn't do nothing."

"I told you Sarah. You see, I told you." He looked

up at the moon and shouted. "Damnit, I told you! It ain't right." He pulled out his grandfather's revolver and pointed at the shining globe in the sky. "I got to do something or I'll die," he said, and pulled the trigger.

Chapter Eleven

"Sure, the Lone Ranger and Tonto."

-Waco

The insurance salesman was feeling rather pleased with himself. He patted his breast pocket unconsciously where he had stuffed a wad of five dollar bills, the first payment on a property protection policy on the Pass Time. He puffed on a big cigar as he steered the '64 Cadillac convertible down the dirt road that headed back to the main highway. He admired the big diamond ring on his finger, confident he would be able to make that month's payment.

It had taken three years, but he knew he'd get those crazy old people in Norte del Sur to buy some kind of a policy eventually. Hell, if he couldn't sell them a policy who could? Didn't he know all the angles. No one got the best of Big Bull Martin. No one. And thanks to a bunch of rich college kids he was able to hike the premium up. Yes, it had been a good day for Bull Martin until suddenly something jumped up in front of the Cadillac. He just caught a glimpse in time as the afternoon sun shown in his eyes. The brakes of the big convertible locked the wheels causing it to swerve on the dirt. He swung the wheel around and veered into the desert. After the car came to a stop, and the dust settled, he found himself staring down the barrel of a revolver.

"Say, what's going on here?" He looked up into two cold blue eyes shaded under the brim of a Stetson hat. The rest of the face was hidden behind a colorful bandana. "What do you think you're doing?" he raged.

Shutup and hand over the money," the voice said from behind the bandana.

"Money? I don't know what you're talking about. You got me wrong, partner. I ain't got no money." He heard the gun cock. "Hey, be careful. That thing might go off."

"The money, Bull. Hand it over."

Martin looked at his diamond ring and frowned. "I'll get you for this." He pulled the wad of worn five dollar bills from his breast pocket and put them into the outstretched hand.

"While you're at it, hand over that ring."

"Not my ring..."

"Hand it over."

"But, it's not paid for..."

"You should have taken out insurance on it..." the voice behind the mask said, leaning into the car and pulling the ring from Martin's finger. "Now, get going."

"You're going to pay for this," the insurance salesman said, starting his engine. "I promise, you're going to pay..." He hit the gas peddle and skidded back onto the road and sped off, leaving a cloud of dust that drifted upward, filtering the sinking sun.

Waco pulled the bandana from his face and smiled. He uncocked the revolver, stuck it back in his belt and trotted off into the desert.

"Well, if it isn't the Lone Ranger," a voice came out of the dusk, sending Waco diving behind a boulder and grabbing for his grandfather's revolver.

"Bang, bang, you're dead white man."

Waco spun around to see Joe standing over him with arms folded.

"Damn. How'd you get here?"

Joe laughed, his white teeth shining from his brown face.

"I've been watching you since you ripped off that insurance guy." He laughed again and extended his hand to Waco to help him up. "Even when we were kids I could track you without you knowing it."

"What are you doing following me around anyway?" Waco said, brushing himself off and sticking his grandfather's revolver back into his belt.

"Sarah saw your face when that insurance guy was at the Pass Time. She asked me to keep an eye on you. You going to get in big trouble you keep this shit up, man."

"That's my business," Waco said.

"You know, for a guy who watches all them cowboy flicks, you sure didn't pull that robbery off too slick. You're lucky that guy didn't have a gun."

"Beginner's luck. You got the wheels? I don't feel like walking."

"Sure compadre." Joe put his arm around his friends shoulder. "You know man, I think you need a partner. Someone who knows what he's doing. After all, if you're going to do this kind of thing, you may as well do it right."

Waco laughed. "Sure, the Lone Ranger and Tonto."

"Fuck off white man. Let's go to Mama Lo's and seal this deal properly."

The two boys walked into the desert. The sun slowly sank beneath the horizon, leaving a glow in the west where the lights of Yuma fifteen miles away were starting to come on.

Jesus lay curled up between two chairs in the undulating light of Mama Lo's that flickered to the rhythm of the gas generator in the rear. Waco and Joe sat at the bar with a half bottle of tequila and a plate of salt and lime wedges between them. The soft snoring of Mama Lo floated in from the rear room which was draped by a colorful Mexican blanket.

"I can't understand why after all these years Sid would use his savings to buy an insurance policy," Waco said, staring into his empty glass. "I mean, he could have bought a new TV. The Pass Time ain't the same without a TV. The folks will die without a TV."

Joe sucked on a piece of lime. "I wish Mama Lo didn't go to sleep. I could use something to eat."

"I figured the best thing that insurance money

could do was buy the folks a new TV," Waco said. "I mean, there's things a man gotta do for his people. You know? All the folks got is their dreams. Sid with his hopes the tourists will come back. Hell, don't nobody care about what happened here no more. I mean, John Wayne, he knew what it was all about, but don't nobody really care no more." He sipped at his empty glass. "Look at the Old Chief. He knows nobody cares. Ain't got nothing but his memories."

Joe looked up from his glass and tried to focus on his friend. "Hum, white man made sure of that," he mumbled, and then struggled with the bottle to pour another drink.

"No man, it's not that," Waco said raising his voice with a thought he couldn't quite put into words. "It's... it's...everything. It's just everything. It don't leave no room for the things that are important..." his voice, trailed off.

Joe looked up, gulped down the tequila, and took a deep breath. Waco looked at him seriously expecting the answer to his thoughts. Joe had always been better with words then he was.

"Brother of mine," Joe said. I think...I think I'm in love..."

"In what?"

"Love. I think..."

"With who?" Waco stammered.

"With...with Maria," Joe answered, trying to make sense of it all.

"You're drunk," Waco shouted and playfully shoved his friend; a push that ordinarily wouldn't have done much, but in Joe's condition it knocked him off the stool and onto the floor. Waco looked down at his friend for a minute, afraid he might have hurt himself until Joe broke into a fit of laughter.

"You drunken Indian," Waco laughed, and extended his hand. Joe took hold of it and pulled Waco from his stool to the floor, and the two of them rolled around laughing uncontrollably until Joe suddenly stopped short:

"I got it," he said.

Waco tried to stop laughing. "What? Got what?"

"I got it. I tell you, I got it."

Waco stopped laughing. He slowly stood up and then helped Joe to his feet. "What the hell are you talking about?"

Joe's eyes were clear. He started to pace up and down the floor. "Sure, it makes sense."

"What the hell are you talking about, man. You're drunk."

"No, Waco. I'm drunk, yes, but I tell you I got an idea." He kept pacing. "You know how Sid is always talking about the tourists coming back, only they never come."

"Yeah. He refuses to believe that Norte del Sur in washed up."

"What makes people come to places?" Joe said.

"I don't know," Waco said. "What?"

I mean, you gave me the idea. Something's got to draw people. And what draws people? Publicity, that's what. Here, look at this." He picked up a copy of the Yuma Star on the counter and flipped through the pages. "Here, here it is. Look at this."

Waco sat back at the bar, still not sure whether

it was the tequila talking, or his friend was really on to something. He looked at the newspaper, trying to focus on where Joe's finger pointed. It was a small article on the fourth page:

Cattle truck bandits still at large.

"See, you robbed Tex and it was in the papers. Now you ripped off that insurance guy, and I'll bet there will be a small story in the Yuma Star about it. But what if we started doing something big...I mean spectacular. What if people thought a real old time outlaw gang was operating down here in Norte del Sur. Man, that would bring the tourists for sure." He stopped pacing and looked at Waco.

"You are drunk," Waco said.

"No man, I'm serious I tell you, it would bring the tourists down in droves."

`Waco thought for a minute. "It would be risky," he said.

"Risky hell. They can only put you in jail once. What's the difference if its for a hundred and fifty dollars or a million. It's all the same, ain't it. Besides, who'd ever suspect us? They already think its the Foley Gang come down from north state."

Waco smiled.

"Me too," a voice came from the corner. "I joining up too. It just like Pancho Villa," Jesus said, yawning.

Chapter Twelve

"...people are going to know about
Norte del Sur."

                                    -Waco

Waco's sleeping eyes were rudely interrupted by a gleam of sun light streaming in through the window, and a blast of hot air blew into the cantina carrying the raspy shriek of Mama Lo's rooster. Memories from the previous night flooded into his aching brain. He must have had a fit of madness. It must have been Grandma Poppy dying. Sure, he had lost his mind—robbing people at gun point. He knew a guy who ended up in jail. He saw himself in stripped clothes behind barred windows.

"Joe...Joe..." he said, shaking his snoring comrade lying on the wooden floor next to him. "I was crazy, man. We can't do it."

Joe didn't move. "Sure man, what ever you say," he

groaned.

Waco shook him again. "Wake up, man."

"What...what.?" Joe rolled over facing him, his eyes still closed .

"Wake up, damnit."

"Okay, okay, I'm, awake. What's going on?" Joe's eyes popped open. He blinked at the bright morning sun.

"It's crazy, man."

"Who's crazy," Joe said, sitting up rubbing his eyes.

"We ain't bandits, Joe. I mean...it's too risky, like you said."

"Sure man, whatever you say," Joe said and rolled back over.

Waco wished Mama Lo had a TV. He wanted to watch a movie; the morning movie must have started all ready. Instead he was stuck with his thoughts and that always troubled him. He closed his eyes only to have visions of his dead grandmother staring at him like they did the night he had found her. How come he couldn't think of her as she was when she was alive? Than she turned into his mother drinking a bottle of whiskey and falling over furniture and screaming how life had cheated her because she was born in Norte del Sur. His mother's eyes turned into the staring brown eyes of Bertha, set in a dark Indian face, while cowboys and cavalry chased down Indians, shooting them dead without any sign of blood from the wounds; and Sid driving the old touring car with the buffalo painted on the side as Suzie, dressed in a white satin dress, threw flowers into an endless hole in the desert while

Mattie kept crying. *'My children are gone...'*

His eyes opened back to the glaring sun, and he stood up. It was going to be another hot day; the kind of day the old folks spent sitting around the TV in the Pass Time drinking Suzie's lemonade as the electric fan blew the heat from one place to another. He could hear Sid and Luke arguing good-naturedly about the coming tourist season until Luke would sneer at Sid; *'Don't nobody care about your damn tours. Norte del Sur is a ghost town just waiting for the rest of us to realize we're all as dead as it is.'* And Sid would challenge his lifelong friend and partner to step outside: *'Who's dead, you old goat. I'll show you who's dead after I kill you...'*

"You're up," Mama Lo said, coming in the front door with a basket of eggs. "You boys drink much tequila last night. I make you some *huevos con mucho* chilies. You see, it make you feel better."

She disappeared into the rear of the cantina. Soon the smell of frying onions, peppers and tomatoes drifted into the room. Jesus jumped up from his bed between the two chairs: "Huevos rancheros," he announced, sniffing the air.

He thinks I'm a coward Waco thought as he looked over at his friend who slowly ate, dipping a fresh corn tortilla into a red chili sauce covered mixed with the orange egg yolk. Joe hadn't taken his eyes off the food since they sat down, not even to say *gracias* to Mama Lo. Jesus gulped down his food as he jabbered about Poncho Villa, and how they would be just like the famous

Mexican general.

"You think I'm chicken, don't you." Waco burst out.

Jesus stopped talking, and Joe slowly looked up from his plate.

"You think I'm chicken cause of what I said... 'cause I said it was crazy."

"I don't think nothing, man," Joe said, taking another steaming tortilla from the covered dish and going back to eating.

"You saw what I done. You know I ain't chicken." Waco said. "It's just that I don't want to get everyone in trouble for...for...I don't know..."

"It don't mean nothing," Joe said, without looking up. "They're just a bunch of old people with stupid dreams. We Indians know about stupid dreams."

Just then a voice rang out from the doorway: "Jesus, there you are."

They looked up. It was Maria. She was in a plain dress and wearing no makeup.

"Why you no come home last night?" she said, walking up to the table. "Waco, where you been? Everybody been worried sick about you. You keeping my brother out all night?"

Joe looked up from his plate again. He unconsciously ran his fingers through his straight black hair, threading out the tangled mats that had formed in his drunken sleep.

"What do you mean, where have I been?" Waco said. "What do you know about it?"

Maria put her arm around his shoulder. "Joe came looking for you," she said, flashing a smile in the Indian boy's direction. "You know he was pretty worried if he come to me."

"Say, how come you was home last night?" Jesus broke in. "You sick?"

Maria straightened up and put her hands proudly on her hips. "I didn't go last night. I quit." she proudly announced.

Waco looked at Joe who had a broad smile on his face.

"I'm going to get a real job." Maria said.

"Maria." Mama Lo said, appearing from the kitchen. "You sick. *Sientate.* I'll bring you some *huevos rancheros.* That fix you up quick."

Waco got out of the ambulance and then watched as it disappeared down the dirt road heading toward the reservation. The wind was kicking up the dust and obscuring the noon sun. It was hot on his face and the wind made his eyes dry. He started walking down the road, past the boarded up buildings. Tumbleweed brushed over his boots, rolled onto the dilapidated porches of the buildings and clung to weather-beaten hitching posts. For the first time in his life Norte del Sur felt like a ghost town; deserted by people and left to rot in the hot desert air of Southern Arizona. Even as he approached the Pass Time the feeling of desertion kept haunting him, like the life that had once filled the final outpost of the town had somehow blown away with the wind. The screen door banged against the doorway as the wind swept through the building. Waco heard the dull thump of his Double Eagle boots as he stepped onto the wooden porch and walked the few short steps to the entrance. The sunlight filtered through the screen door, highlighting the dust that whirled around inside. He grabbed hold of the banging door and held it for a moment before entering.

The desert had begun its creep into the Pass Time, settling onto the bar, the tables and the floor. Empty beer cans and broken glass where swept into small piles like so many tiny mountains. In the corner the TV sat silent, its face shattered. A voice came from the large chair where Bertha always sat facing the TV:

"That you Sheriff? You catch them cowards. Your job, Sheriff. You catch em."

"It's me, Bertha. It's Waco."

The Indian woman looked up at the boy. "They busted the TV, Sheriff. They busted the TV and you ought to do something. It's your job Sheriff. Somebody's gotta do something, and you're the Sheriff." She looked back at the shattered TV and began playing with the on/off knob, clicking it back and forth as if the mere act would somehow make it work again.

"Bertha, where is everyone?" Waco said, knowing he wouldn't get an answer. The old Indian woman stared into the smashed TV screen, switching the knob on and off, on and off. He slowly walked out of the Pass Time, running his hand across the dusty bar as he passed it. He made his way up the small hill leading to the cemetery. A lone figure was standing in front of a grave. The marker was worn by the wind and the writing had long ago become unreadable.

"Sid, what're you doing? Where's everyone?" Waco said.

The man turned around. His face was drawn and tired. "Waco."

"What're you doing, Sid?"

The old man turned back to the faded wooden marker. "Me and Martha was having a little talk, Waco. I told her what's happened. I told her it's all done and finished here in Norte del Sur. She been arguing with me. You know...that's how women are; always looking on the bright side. You know. I told her people don't care no more about what happened here. People don't care about the past no more."

Waco looked at the marker. It was Sid's wife. "What's she tell you, Sid?"

Sid looked up at the boy, a slight smile crossed his face. "Says people do care. Says all they need is to know, and then they'll come back to Norte del Sur." He looked back at the grave and shook his head sadly. "Always was an optimist, you know. Started the Optimists' Club in Yuma, you know."

"She's right, Sid," Waco said, putting his hand on the old man's shoulder. "And people are going to know about Norte del Sur. I promise you. People going to know." He took the money from the holdup and pressed it into Sid's hand.

"Buy another TV, Sid."

"Where'd this come from, son?"

"Insurance money, Sid." Waco smiled and walked away.

Chapter Thirteen

"... just like in the movies..."
-Jesus

Joe sat at the wooden table smiling as he cleaned a double barreled shotgun and listened as Waco tried to convince him of the reasons why they should go ahead with their original plan. Joe had made up his mind before Waco had second thoughts. Going on the war path was part of his heritage; it was in his blood. There wasn't much of a future for an Indian off the reservation. His wasn't a wealthy tribe, and he hated poverty programs and the do-gooders who flooded the reservation to "help" the poor Indians. One summer he traveled to Utah to work in the uranium mines; but it didn't take long before he realized that would be a sure road to an early grave, not that he feared death, but the slow radiation poisoning from the mines wasn't his idea of a' noble way to die. There wasn't much for Joe. Unlike his brother, he didn't like the idea of taking orders from a bunch of white men, and he had seen too many of his friends return from Vietnam wounded in their bodies or their minds. Some returned in pine boxes. The Old Chief had said when his brother went off, *'Only crazy man go fight across the great water. A warrior fight for honor and horses. White man's war is bull.'* So, while Waco sat across from him trying to convince him that becoming bandits to help the old people was really a good idea, Joe had already known he had nothing to lose. Hadn't he said that the night before— at least he seemed to remember he said it, although that night and the morning after were still a bit hazy. But it was something he had been ready for all his life; a chance to do something that meant something. His people may have surrendered to the white man, but as far as he was concerned, he hadn't signed a peace treaty with the U.S. Government, so why should he obey its rules.

"You're right," he said, interrupting Waco's speech. "We got to do it. It's the right thing."

"I knew you'd see it my way," Waco said, and the two boys sat at the table looking at each other for a minute as the desert wind slapped against the bare wooden walls of old deserted cabin near the border. Finally, Waco broke the silence:

"What should we do?"

Joe put the shotgun on the table. "Beats me, but we'd better start off with something easy after what I saw you do with that insurance guy. If that guy had a gun you'd be dead, and I'm too young to die."

Suddenly the door swung open. "*Viva la causa!*" It was Jesus. "*Viva Villa!*"

"Something real easy," Joe said, as he smiled at the Mexican boy.

A car appeared out of the glaring watery mirage from the black asphalt highway, giving the impression it was rising from a distant lake. Joe looked up at the hill where Jesus stood watch. Two flashes from a mirror catching the bright sun struck his eyes .

"Looks like a good one," he shouted to Waco who stood some hundred yards away where an old dirt construction road forked off the main highway and veered behind some rocks to a dead end. He dragged a road block onto the highway with an arrow and the hand lettered words "detour." He ran back down the dirt road where Waco waited, and then glanced back up at the hill. Three flashes hit his eyes:

"Shit, something's wrong," he said to himself and ran back to the highway. He saw there were two cars as they both rose over a mound in the highway and then disappeared back into a depression. Behind the new Chrysler was a white police car. He quickly dragged the construction sign off the road, knocked it onto its side, and ducked behind a clump of sage brush just as the two cars sped past. He wiped the sweat from his face as he came back out onto the highway and shook his fist toward the hill where Jesus hid. He then walked back up the dirt road to Waco when two flashes from the mirror again hit his eyes. "Shit, you do it this time," he said.

Waco gave him a dirty look, and then ran down the dirt road to the highway where he dragged out the detour sign, the sweat pouring down his face from beneath the wide brimmed hat. He looked down the highway just as two shiny new cars appeared on the rise in the road. He ran back to where Joe waited, holding the shotgun.

"They're coming...two of them," he said. "Looks like good pickin's; a Cadi convertible and some kinda fancy foreign job."

Joe mopped his face with a handkerchief. "Man, this is harder than work," and than wrapped the handkerchief around his head so it covered his nose and mouth.

Four flashes from Jesus signaled that the cars had turned off the highway. The two boys slipped behind the rocks on both sides of the road. Waco pulled his grandfather's revolver from his belt. Joe held the shotgun at ready. They could see the dust rising into the air as the cars approached...

"It was just like in the movies," Jesus said excitedly as Sarah sat on the old couch in Poppy Merkin's house, her arms folded tightly across her chest. "Joe jumped out with his gun, and Waco jumped out with his pistol, and that first car stopped so quick that the other one banged right into it. Is true, right Joe?"

Joe sat at the kitchen table in Grandma Merkin's front room with the shotgun laying in front of him. He looked up.

"So," Sarah said. "What happened?" only the way she said it, it was obvious she was irritated and not impressed.

"So," Joe said, "I told them to get out of their cars, and this big guy jumps out of the Cadi, leaving this blond woman sitting with her mouth wide open..."

"Yeah," Jesus interrupted. "You should have seen her, Sarah. She had this dress, you could see her chichis hangin' out, and everything..."

"I get the picture," Sarah said.

"'What the hell...' the guy starts to say," Joe continued, "but before he can say anymore, the guy in the the foreign job gets out shouting, 'What the hell's the matter with you, fella! Look what you done to my car,' 'cause he hasn't seen us yet, and the two of them start in arguing over whose fault it was."

Jesus interrupted again. "And the lady with her chichis hanging out, she starts to scream, and then Joe fires that shotgun and tells them all to shut up."

Suddenly Waco, who had been quietly standing in the corner, started to laugh. "Sarah, you wouldn't have believed it. Joe sticks his shotgun right in the big guy's gut, and the guy says, 'You can't do this to me. Don't know who I am.' And Joe says, 'we don't give a shit who you are. This is a stickup.'"

Everyone looked at him. It was the first time Sarah had ever heard him laugh. Waco just never laughed, and it made Sarah smile. Than Joe began laughing too.

"So the other man turns to the big guy and shouts: 'Shut that bitch up before these people shoot all of us.' And the big guy, he don't know what to do; quiet the woman down, or put his hands up..." Waco continued.

"And the lady with her chichis hanging out, she starts screaming again, 'they're going to rape me,'" Jesus said, giggling.

Sarah couldn't contain herself. It was all so ridiculous that she burst out laughing.

"Rape her?" Joe laughed. "She was old enough to be my mother ..."

"And ugly," Jesus threw in, and then the laughter overcame them all and no one could speak for several minutes.

Finally Sarah controlled herself and wiped the tears from her eyes. "So, you brave *bandidos*, what did you get out of all this?"

Waco and Joe looked at each other and their gaiety quickly dissolved. Waco took a handful of crumbled up bills from his pocket and laid them on the table. Sarah stood up and counted the money. "A hundred and fifty dollar? That's all?"

"Damn Sar," Waco said. "All they had was credit cards."

"You dummies could have got yourselves killed, and all you got was a hundred and fifty dollars? You call yourselves outlaws, and all you got was a lousy hundred and fifty dollars?"

"We did it for the folks, Sar," Waco said in a pleading voice.

Sarah just stood there and shook her head. Then she gentle put her hand on Waco's cheek. "I know why you did it Waco, and I'm proud of you guys. But next time, I'm coming along. This outfit needs someone with brains. That's obvious."

"Hey, we don't need no girls in the gang." Jesus shouted.

"Shut up," Waco said. "Sarah's one of us."

Sarah kissed Waco on the cheek. "If we're going to do this, we're going to do it right."

Chapter Fourteen

"... we could all get murdered in our beds."
-Suzie

Sid sat in his rocking chair in front of the Pass Time thumbing through the *Yuma Star,* a smile on his face as the sound of "*As the World Turns*" blasted from the new 25 inch color TV inside. Perhaps his wife was right. Perhaps things were going to get better. He flipped the newspaper to the front page. His eyes opened wide at the lead story, and then he jumped from his seat:

"Luke," he shouted. "Luke, take a look at this, would ya."

"What are you shouting about," Luke said, emerging from the front door with a broom in his hand. He let the screen slam behind him. "How'm I going to get this place cleaned up you keep yelling at me. I could use some help you know."

"Look at this," Sid said, shoving the newspaper under Luke's nose. "Just look at this..."

Luke glanced at the newspaper, and then grabbed it from Sid's hands and inspected it closely. "Hey, that's the sonofabitch what wrecked our place."

"Yeah, he's that bastard Rowdy Boyle's kid. See, that's Boyle there who got held up yesterday down the road. And look, it talks about Norte del Sur."

"That's him all right. Ain't he the guy that screwed us several years back?"

"Damn right. Weren't for him we'd a been a State Historical Site. Bastard."

"Oh well, that was a long time ago." Luke looked back into the paper. "Look, says: 'the robbery took place only one mile from the ghost town of Norte del Sur where Mexican bandits and highway men once roamed freely back and forth across the Mexican border, earning the small town a lasting place in Arizona history'."

"It says that Luke?" Sid said quickly forgetting his old grudge.

"And it goes on: 'It now appears the vicinity around Norte del Sur has become the haven of the notorious Foley gang, last known to operate in North State...'"

"What's all the excitement?" Suzie said, joining them on the porch in a neat white sun dress.

The two men didn't look up from the paper. Luke

kept reading, "... 'and once again bringing Norte del Sur into notoriety following the daring daytime hold-up of State Representative Rowdy Boyle and a woman who has asked that her name be withheld. Also robbed was...'"

"Damn Luke, Suzie, you know what this means?"

"It means we could all get murdered in our bed, that's what it means," Suzie said.

"No, no. It means things are looking up. It's just like my Martha said. I'm telling you..."

"Oh Sid, you're still dreaming," Luke said. "It don't mean nothing. Don't nobody care." He turned around and walked back into the Pass Time.

Suzie put her hand on Sid's shoulder. "Don't get your hopes up old man."

"Who're you calling old man you old bag," Sid said good-naturedly. "Trouble with you people is you ain't got no faith, that's all. You got to be optimistic in this here world."

Suzie put her hand on his arm and pressed against him as she kissed him on the cheek. "That's right honey, things are looking up."

He felt the heat of her lips on his face and her body against his. It had been a long time since he had felt a woman this close. But the moment was rudely disrupted by a car speeding down the dirt road, kicking up a cloud of dust.

"See," Sid said. "Folks are coming already. What'd I tell you."

Suzie put on her glasses and looked down the road. "Sure. It's only Deputy Hank. Wouldn't count on him spending the night if I was you, Sid."

"Well," Sid said, "least wise we're having more excitement around here than we've had in a long time. Better see what he wants."

"Probably hasn't got anything else to do," Suzie said, irritated by the interruption.

The car pulled up in front of the Pass Time with the dust rolling over it and floating into the hot air. Hank stepped out of the car and dusted himself off.

"Howdy Sid. Suzie." He stepped onto the porch, took off his hat and ran a handkerchief over his forehead. "Hot enough for you?"

"No more than usual this time of year," Sid said, sitting back down in the rocking chair.

"Get you a beer, Hank," Suzie asked.

"On duty, Suzie. Got a pop?"

"Lemonade's best I can do."

"Thanks Suzie. That'll be fine."

Suzie went back into the Pass Time as Luke came back out.

"Hank."

"Luke, how's things?"

"Same old same old," Luke said. "Suppose you've come about the robberies. Darnedest thing."

"Matter of fact, that's what I'm here about."

Sid looked at the newspaper. "Says here it's the Foley gang."

"Yeah," Hank said. "That's what the Sheriff thinks."

"Come on Hank," Luke laughed. "Old man Foley retired three years ago. Son's in college last I heard, and those other two bums used to run with him..."

"'Sides Hank, " Sid interrupted. "Foley never did no

armed robberies. Rustled cattle was all."

"Sure, sure, I know that," Hank said. "Told the Sheriff as much, but he insisted it was Foley. Boyle was coming down hard on him. Was Boyle what got him the job down here. Fact is, all we got on these guys doin' the jobs is one of 'em wears Double Eagle boots. Saw the same prints where Boyle was robbed as I saw at the scene where Tex's truck was ditched. You fellas wouldn't happen to know anyone wears Double Eagles would you?"

Luke looked down at Sid who kept his eyes glued to the newspaper, then shrugged. "Can't say as I do, Hank."

"Well, Boyle got a surprise coming." Sid said, looking up from the paper. "Was his kid what tore up our place here and attacked that Mexican gal..."

"What!" Hank said.

"You heard him, Hank," Luke said, grabbing the paper from Sid's hands and thrusting it at the deputy and banging his finger at the picture on the front page.

"That kid's the one...Boyle's kid!"

Hank mopped his brow with the handkerchief again. "The shit you say."

Sid stood up. "And what are you going to do about it?"

Hank fell into the rocking chair. "Wait a minute boys. Just hold on here."

Suzie came out with a glass and handed it to the deputy. "Hank. Nice and cold."

"Thanks," he said, and took a long drink. He looked back at Sid and Luke. "That's a mighty serious charge you fellas are making. I came out here to ask if you seen anyone suspicious, and now you're going to tell me that Rowdy Boyle's kid is guilty of tearing up your place, and maybe attempted rape..."

"Try assault with a deadly weapon too," Luke said.

"Wait a minute...just hold on. Are you saying you fellas are prepared to press charges against State Representative Boyle's kid?"

"Damn right we are," Sid said.

Hank stood up, finished off the glass of lemonade and handed the glass back to Suzie. He put his hat back on his head. "Listen fellas. I ain't got long to retirement, and this kinda thing... well, you could make a lot of trouble with this thing."

"You saying you ain't going to arrest the kid?" Luke said.

"Wait a minute," Hank said, edging back toward the car. "Let me take this up with the Sheriff, but I an tell you right now what he'll say. You're talking about some serious political shit here.

"Hank, we knowed each other for a lot of years," Sid said. "You know what I mean. Are you telling us you'd ignore this 'cause it might cost you your job?" Sid said, knowing it was an unfair question as soon as he asked it. Sure Hank would try to ignore it, or brush it under the rug if he could. Thirty years a deputy, and passed over for sheriff, with only a couple of years left to pension, he'd probably do the same thing. But it was his place that got busted up, and Sid had no love for Boyle ever since the State Representative from Yuma ignored his request to have Norte del Sur designated a historical landmark, and when he had personally contacted the Representative was told, "don't nobody care about your bunch of shacks in the desert. Just be thankful we still deliver water out there." So, even though he counted Hank as a friend, he couldn't resist pressing the issue.

But, as Hank inched his way to his car stammering, "I'll look into it fellas. I promise, I'll look into it...." another car approached down the main street through the center of town, and everyone's attention was distracted because it was a station wagon filled with people.

Hank slid back into his car and started the engine.

"You see that you do," Sid shouted, as Hank drove away, and the station wagon pulled up into the spot in front of the Pass Time where Hank had pulled out.

"This Norte del Sur?" the man in the station wagon asked, sticking his head out the window.

Sid, Luke and Suzie stared in the car; wife, four kids, a pile of luggage, and Ohio license plate. Tourists!

"It said on the sign this was the way to Norte del Sur," the man repeated.

"Uh, yeah, this is Norte del Sur," Sid stammered. "What can I do for you?"

"Well, we was on our way to Mexicali and we saw the newspaper article said this is a historical spot. Thought we'd check it out. There a motel or something?"

"Motel?" Sid stammered. "I...well..."

Luke stepped in. "Sure thing, partner. You're at the right place. Got cabins and guided tours. You and your family come right in. Got fresh lemonade while we get your cabin fixed up."

"Right," Sid said. "This is Norte del Sur, the toughest town in the old west..."

"Bring the kids in," Suzie said. "Got a new color TV. Should be a Western coming on soon. Bet they'll like that."

Chapter Fifteen

"it had been a dream"

-Suzie

Suzie talked all the way Into Yuma, but Sarah wasn't listening; she was planning. Suzie was used to the fact that the girl didn't listen to her, but that didn't stop her from talking, and on this day she had a lot to talk about:

"...and I'm going to have to tell Juanita to do my hair extra special nice today," she said, "because we have guests. My, you should have seen Sid. Never seen him so excited; well, not in a lot of years anyway. And Luke, he just went up to those people and said, 'of course we have rooms,' while Sid stood there flabbergasted. And Mattie, my goodness, her eyes just lit up. She couldn't believe that people had actually come back to Norte del Sur, just like in the old days. Bertha, well you know Bertha."

And so it went all the way into Yuma where Sarah pulled up in front of the Flower of the Desert Beauty Salon where Suzie had been having her hair done every week since Sarah could remember.

Everyone knew that Suzie was in love with Sid; everyone put Sid who still mourned his wife who had passed away from influenza over eight years ago. But that didn't stop Suzie from fixing herself up and hoping Sid would notice. Besides, she liked her time alone with Sarah, Mattie and Luke's granddaughter. Having no children of her own, she looked on Sarah as if she was her own child.

"Come on Sarah, let me have your hair done up for you. You're such a pretty gal."

But Sarah had other things on her mind. "Not today, Auntie."

She knew that all the excitement over Norte del Sur would last only as long as there was attention drawn to the small town, and, much as she believed in law and order, she knew Waco and Joe were determined to continue their lawless path. She tried to deny the thrill she had felt when the boys were telling her about of the holdup, convincing herself that the reason she insisted on joining them was for the sake of the old folks, and that it was obvious the boys needed her help or they would end up in prison for sure. Maybe Waco was right. Maybe sometimes folks had to do what was right even if that meant going against the law.

Their next job had to be a big one; something that would make headline news and would be picked up by TV news. It could be their last job. But they would have to score big. It would take a lot of money to fix up the Pass Time. The cabins needed new furniture and linen., and most of swamp pumps were busted. Air condition would be needed. The restaurant and bar need to be modernized. The whole place needed to be polished. Maybe, if they scored big enough, they could even put in a swimming pool. It was something she had only be able to dream of in the past.

But there was another reason; there was Waco, the boy she always thought of as a brother, but who she found, over the past several months, feeling something more than sisterly affection. She could see the way he looked at her and knew he was feeling it too. They had always been drawn together; the children of Norte del Sur who had been left in their grandparents' care while their own parents had run off.

Sarah didn't remember her mother. Grandma Mattie said she had left when Sarah was a small child, but that someday she would come back. Sarah didn't care one way or the other. It was hard thinking about a person who she never knew, and who had thought so little of her that she had abandoned her. As for Grandpa Luke, well, he just never spoke of her. But, that was the way it was in Norte del Sur.

After dropping Suzie off she headed for the strip on the highway leading north out of Yuma. She cruised slowly past the string of stucco motels: The Yucca Motel, The Desert Inn, The Wild Horse Motel, The Cactus

Motel, until she spotted what she was after. It was a extra long old Cadillac limousine parked in front of the Dew Drop Inn with the words "Bernstein's Wild West Shows" painted in large letters across the side. She had the next robbery planned in her head, and Bernstein's Wild West Shows was an important part of it. She pulled into the driveway, parked next to the limo, and grabbed a bag of tools from under the seat.

Chapter Sixteen

"...everyone, up against the wall."
-Joe

There was still a chill over the desert as the first crack of gold flared over the horizon, soon followed by the orange globe which popped up from the desert like a gigantic cactus plant, turning the grey sky into a sea of blue swallowing up the last remaining stars.

Joe and Waco sat huddled over a small one burner Coleman stove and warmed their hands around cups of steaming coffee. Jesus sat bundled up in the front seat of the ambulance that stood on a small rise next to the dry stream bed they had used as a road to where they waited on Sarah to arrive. She said she had a plan.

"Where is she?" Waco said, staring into the steaming cup. "I don't like this waiting."

"Said she'd be here," Joe said, sipping from his cup.

"I still don't like this," Waco said. "Wish she'd told us what the plan is. I don't like it."

"Hey man, cool it. Sarah's smarter than you and me put together. Said she'd be here, and she'll be here. 'Sides, after the last job, she couldn't do no worse."

"Yeah, you're right about that. I just don't want her getting into no trouble," Waco said.

Soon they heard a rumbling off in the distance, and then a cloud of dust rose from the gully. Sarah appeared astride a horse and trailing two others.

"Boy, look at that girl ride," Jesus shouted from the ambulance window.

Sarah reined in the horses and jumped off with the agility of an experienced rider.

"What the hell are these?" Waco said

Sarah caught her breath. It was steaming as was that of the three horses as they snorted from their noses. Sarah patted one of them.

"They're horses. Never seen one before?" she laughed.

Joe smiled as Waco stood his ground with his hands on his hips with a stern look. "I know what they are. Where did you get them?"

"From the Bar Q. It was easy. We need them for the job," Sarah said.

You stole them!" Waco heard his voice rise. "That's horse stealing!"

Joe burst out laughing.

Sarah found herself with her arms lovingly around Waco's neck. She had to stretch to her tip toes to reach him, and she thought how she hadn't noticed how tall he had gotten.

"They hang people for horse stealing," Waco said, feeling awkward and not knowing what to do with his hands as the girl's body pressed next to him.

"You silly boy," Sarah said in his ear.

"We're about to commit armed robbery and you're worried about stealing a few horses?" Joe said through his laughter.

Sarah kissed Waco on the cheek, and then pulled away from him and went back to the horses. She turned around. She was all business now.

"The horses are from the Bar Q Dude Ranch. You guys know it. We're going to hold it up. It's all set."

"All right," Jesus shouted. "We going to hit the rich gringos."

"Not you Jesus," Sarah said. "You stay with the truck. "

"Ah Sarah..."

"That's important," Joe added. "Someone's gotta be lookout."

"Yeah," Jesus said. "That's important, man."

"Besides," Joe said. "You get caught the *migra* will send you back to Mexico."

"Yeah," Jesus said.

Waco smiled at Sarah. In that moment they both realized that they were no longer just childhood friends, but had become a man and a woman, and in that one glance things had forever changed between them.

"So," Joe said. "What's the plan?"

"Huh," Sarah said, forcing her eyes away from Waco. 'The plan. Yes." She walked over to the stove and poured a cup of coffee. Her breath blew white off the hot black liquid. The others gathered around her. "Every year they stage a holdup at the Bar Q. It makes the tourists happy...you know, real old west stuff. Well, it's simple. Today's the day for the holdup. So, we're going to hold em up. Therefore, the horses."

"I don't get it Sarah," Waco said. "If they stage a holdup, they must have some actors or something do it."

"They do; Bernstein's Wild West Shows." Sarah smiled. "But they're going to have a problem getting here today. Trust me."

"What if they only have credit cards?" Waco said.

"They have gambling at the Bar Q. There'll be plenty of cash." Sarah answered.

Joe and Waco looked at each other. "Sounds good to me," Joe said .

"Well, if we're going to do this thing let's do it," Waco said.

"You got a gun for me?" Sarah said, pinning her hair up as Waco watched her admiringly. "Waco?"

Waco blushed. He knew she had caught him watching her. "I don't think you should come," he stammered, suddenly feeling protective of her. "I don't..."

"What do you mean," Sarah said. "Of course I'm coming. It's my plan and you ain't going to bungle it."

Joe pulled a Winchester repeating rifle from the ambulance and tossed it to her, "Here. It belongs to the Chief. Says he used it on the white eyes."

Waco took the rifle from Sarah. She looked at him

accusingly, and then smiled as he said, "Here Sar, I'll check it out for you."

The Bar Q, formally the King Ranch, was a large spread in the middle of the desert where thousands of head of cattle once grazed. According to Sid it was the largest cattle ranch west of Texas. Also, according to Sid—the local expert on that part of Arizona—the ranch was originally started by a disinherited son of the famous King Cattle Ranch family of Texas. He had rustled several hundred head from his family and moved to the Arizona Territory to stake out his own fortune. But around 1920 the once sparse grazing land had dried up and returned to the desert, and cattle rustlers had taken their toll on the ranch until King gave up and abandoned the place, moving to Los Angeles where he made a fortune in the wholesale meat business, also according to Sid, and since no one knew different it was accepted as fact.

What everyone did know was that now the King Ranch was the Bar Q, and the only thing raised there were cocktails at five by the tourists that came for "rest and relaxation among the sage brush." The advertisements boasted seclusion and meant it. The only access to the Bar Q was by private plane or a twenty mile dirt road that was impassable in the winter except by horse or four wheel drive.

Sarah knew the place well. She had worked there one season as a maid until one of the guests came on to her and she was fired for punching him in the face. In her imagination she had plotted a thousand ways to get even with the swishy manager who fired her, but never thought she'd get the chance. She smiled to herself as the three bandits rode up to the front of the ranch. Revenge would be sweet.

Those guests who woke up would be just getting ready for breakfast. Some would be at the bar having a Bloody Mary to ease the headaches left over from the night before. Some more ambitious guests would have just returned from the morning ride, but judging from the number of horses in the stables when Sarah borrowed the three for the job, there weren't many takers that morning. She felt her heart pounding as they dismounted the horses and tied them to the hitching post in front of the main entrance of the large ranch house. Several people were making their way from the surrounding cabins, and walked past them.

"Morning," Joe smiled at two attractive middle aged women who must have been up early enough for the morning ride, but had spent their time instead putting on their makeup and squeezing into jeans that were two sizes too small.

Sarah pushed Waco who was following the women with his eyes as they wiggled up the steps to the front porch.

"Come on you clowns. We going to do this or what?" She pulled her bandana up around her nose so it covered her face.

Waco and Joe did the same. Waco pulled his pistol from the belt under his jacket and Joe got his shotgun from the saddle on the horse and checked the chambers. Sarah took the Winchester.

"Remember," she said "they're expecting a show so don't shoot nobody no matter what happens."

"Don't worry Sarah," Joe said. "We ain't looking to hurt no one." He headed up the stairs, followed by Waco. Sarah took a deep breath. This was it.

"Alright everyone, up against the wall. This is a stickup!" Joe shouted, as Sarah and Waco moved into the combination bar and dining room, herding people together with their guns.

"Get moving if you know what's good for you," Waco sneered as he poked the pistol into the fat gut of a middle-aged man who was laughing with a bleached blond woman wearing a ridiculous looking cowboy hat.

"Say, take her easy fella. I'm payin' your salary here."

Sarah held her gun on the rest of the guests who had obediently followed instructions as they played along with "Oohs," and "Aahs" and "please don't shoots," and then she turned toward the fat guy Waco had just poked. "You heard what the man said fatty. Move it!"

Suddenly a voice came over a loudspeaker throwing a momentary chill of fear down Sarah's back; and then she recognized it; high pitched with a slight lisp and Southern accent, and she could hear it saying, "You don't have what it takes to work at the Bar Q young lady." only this time it said, "Attention everybody. Everyone please come to the main dining room for an authentic wild west holdup..."

Joe had the shotgun pointed at the thin manager whose sparse hair fell over narrow shoulders. A western tie was pulled tight around his skinny neck that stuck out of a gaudy western shirt, and he kept wringing his hands. "And bring all your valuables," he said into the microphone that sat on the reception desk in the lobby.

"Just cash," Joe said.

"Yes, of course. Just cash. These are tough hombres." He looked up at Joe. "Say, you're not the regular guys."

"No," Joe said. "They got held up." He laughed at his own joke as the manager wrung his hands, and then laughed nervously.

"Held up," he said. "I get it. You boys make this good, and there'll be a bonus in it for you. You could have worn something a little more flashy though, you know, with frills and things. The other boys always looked so..so..."

"Never mind," Joe snapped. "Just open the safe."

"The safe?" the manager said. "The other boys never did that."

"Oh look, Bob," a grey haired woman said to her equally grey haired husband as they walked into the lobby from outside. "It's a real holdup, just like on TV."

"I don't think I should open the..." the manager said, but a blast from Joe's shotgun changed his mind.

"Oh my, they are desperate hombres," he said to the old couple, and began spinning the dial on the safe behind the desk as bits of plaster dropped from the ceiling where Joe had fired.

"Say, you're not using real bullets," the manager asked, his voice a little shaky.

"Realism," Joe said.

By then Sarah and Waco were already making a collection from the people in the dining room. Waco kept them covered as Sarah took wallets and purses and dumped them into a shopping bag.

"Say, there's five hundred bucks in this wallet," the same man with the fat gut protested. "When we getting these things back?"

"That's not my department, pal," Sarah said, snatching the wallet from his hands and tossing it into the bag.

"Oh, don't be such a spoiled sport," his bleached blonde companion said just as the shotgun blast reverberated through the room. "Golly, this is exciting."

Joe marched the old couple and the manager into the room.

"You finished here," he said.

"All but these two," Waco replied, referring to the old couple.

"These two? Why they're my partners, ain't you?" Joe said, putting his arms around the two old people who had silly smiles on their faces, proud to be befriended by the "outlaws."

Sarah walked up to the manager and stuck her rifle into his ribs. "What about this one," she said. "You get him? Empty your pockets, dude, or I'll blow a hole in you..."

"Oh, that's good. And I do believe this one's a lady outlaw." The manager kept wringing his hands. "Marvelous. Simply marvelous."

Just then Jesus appeared in the lobby, "Hey, you guys," he motioned to them.

Joe went into the lobby, and then returned. "We got to go," he said quietly.

But as they turned to leave, the manager grabbed

them.

"Aren't you going to shot me?" he whispered. "You've got to shot me..."

Joe and Waco looked at each other in amazement, but Sarah was ready for her cue; she had seen the act. She pointed the rifle at the manager's head and cocked it. For a split second the manager saw a look in the girl's eye that sent a chill down his spin. Then the gun exploded and he felt the bullet whiz over his head. He stood motionless for a minute as the three bandits disappeared out the door. Then, assuring himself that he was not really shot, he fell to the floor:

"They got me."

The ambulance was sitting outside the ranch house with the engine running. "Come on," Jesus shouted. "They'll be here in a few minutes."

"What's going on?" Sarah said.

"Your bad guy actors are on their way. Waco, shoot the phone line," Joe said.

"Right," Waco said, drawing his pistol and firing at the telephone pole. The bullet missed. Again he fired, and again the bullet missed its target, then fired again, missing each time.

"Damn."

Then one bullet from Sarah's rifle took the line down. Waco frowned, and pushed the smirking Sarah into back of the ambulance. Joe slammed his foot onto the gas Pedal and the ambulance took off into the desert. He tuned his head toward Jesus.

"Where's you learn to drive?"

The boy just shrugged.. "It's not hard."

Waco slouched down next to Sarah.

"Don't feel bad, Waco. The telephone was out of range for the .45"

"It didn't make him feel any better.

"Four thousand five hundred and sixty, four thousand five hundred and eighty, four thousand six hundred..." Sarah sat at the small dining room table at Poppy Merkin's ranch with a pile of money and wallets in front of her.

Waco sat on the arm of the old couch in the adjoining living room. *"The Man Who Shot Liberty Valence"* was on the small black and white TV. It was one of his favorite westerns—John Wayne and Jimmy Stewart—but Waco wasn't able to concentrate as his eyes continually drifted over to Sarah at the table.

"These people don't believe in nothing smaller than twenties," Sarah said without looking up. "Makes it easy to count. Now, the hundreds. One, two, three, four, five—I wonder why Joe was so eager to take Jesus home? Never saw him in such a hurry—Six, seven, eight..."

"Well, maybe there's something across the border he's interested in." Waco slid off the arm of the couch, switched off the TV, and walked over to the table behind Sarah and put his hands on her shoulders.

"Don't bother me, Waco. I'll lose count. Nine, one thousand." She placed the bills into a neat pile, and then looked over her shoulder at Waco and smiled. "So, what would that be?"

"What?"

"What he would be interested in across the border."

"If I tell you, you got to promise not to say anything." He let loose of her shoulders and walked back to the living room and stared at the blank screen of the TV for a minute. It was hard for him to think about ...Joe and Maria...love. It made him uneasy.

"Well?" Sarah said. "You got me curious. What is it?"

Waco turned around and looked her straight in the eyes. "I think Joe's in love." The word love almost caught in his throat. He hadn't had many occasions to use it, and the love he felt for his grandmother and for the old folks he never expressed in words. Words like *love* weren't used much by the people of Norte del Sur. But there was another reason it was hard to say. He knew that the words "in love" were different, and what he was feeling for Sarah—and not knowing whether she was "in love" with him—made it all the harder to say.

Sarah rose from the chair and went to him, putting her arm around his shoulder. "I'm sorry, Waco."

He looked at her. "Sorry? Why?"

I thought you and Maria...well, I always thought you two..."

"What? What makes you think it's Maria?"

"It sure isn't Mama Lo makes you hang out down there so much."

"No," he said, standing up. "Me and Maria are just friends. Kinda like you and me, only..."

"Only what Waco?"

"Only..." Waco hesitated.

"I know, Waco," Sarah said softly. "It's all right."

"No, we were...I mean we are. Really!" He was getting angry, and walked away from her. "I don't love Maria," he said excitedly. "I love you..." he stopped short, realizing what he just said and it scared him. How would she react? He was too embarrassed to turn back to Sarah

The room filled with silence, the kind of silence that only exists in the desert—total stillness as if the world itself had stopped moving.

"What did you say?" Sarah finally managed to force from between her lips. Her heart pounded. "Did you say that you love me?" she said in what seemed to her a squeaky little voice that made her blush in shame. "Waco?"

He turned around abruptly. "I'm sorry, Sar. I shouldn't have said that. I mean..."

She went up to him and took his hands in hers. "Waco..."

He looked down at their clasped hands. All he could think of was that his were sweating and it made him self-conscious.

"Waco..."

"I...I don't know, Sar. I..."

She rose to her tip toes and gently kissed his lips. For a moment they looked into each other's eyes. Waco let go of her hands and reached around her waist, pulling her tightly next to him, searching out her lips which drew to him like a magnet. She instinctively parted them, slowly drawing his tongue to her. They explored each other this way for what seemed like an eternity, their lips clinging tightly, their tongues eagerly exploring, until finally they just stood there, their bodies pressed tightly together. They stared into one another's eyes in wonderment, silently seeking an answer to what was happening between them.

"Waco....what do we do now?" Sarah said in a low voice he had never heard before; a voice which further aroused a longing in him.

"I...I'm not sure," he stammered.

"Didn't you ever do anything before?

"I..." he was embarrassed to admit he had never been with a woman. But he knew any lies he might make up—the kind all boys tell each other—would be seen through by Sarah. "No Sar," he admitted.

She smiled at him and again brushed her lips against his. "I love you, Waco..."

Chapter Seventeen

*"I figure it's a local bunch. From what
I hear sounds like youngsters."*

-Deputy Hank

Morrison slammed the phone down. Hank could tell he was agitated, and he knew the reason. But since he was still only the deputy he decided it wasn't his responsibility, so he sat quietly across from the Sheriff with a smile on his face. It wasn't like when Bob Garrett was Sheriff. Garrett was old school. He had earned his position as sheriff by the ballot and didn't owe political favors to anyone. Morrison was a political appointee and owed favors to everyone, and Representative Rowdy Boyle had just reminded the Sheriff of the fact in no uncertain terms. When Garrett was Sheriff Hank pretty much ran his own show. *"I been Sheriff of this here county for a lot a years,"* he used to tell Hank, *"and you been around much of that time.*

You don't need me to tell you how to do your job, and I don't need you botherin' me all the time. Get enough of that from the rookies they keep sending me from the Academy. Trouble with this law enforcement nowadays is it's all politics and bureaucracy."

Morrison swung around in his swivel chair and shot an angry look at Hank.

What you smilin' at, deputy?"

"Nothin' sheriff. Finished my report on the Bar Q case. It's on your desk."

"I see it. I want to hear it from your mouth. It's bad enough I got Boyle on my ass over that first robbery. Now it looks like he owns part of the Bar Q, and he's screamin' for results." Morrison flipped through the file folder on the desk.

"Looks like Foley got a woman runnin' with him."

"Investigation don't seem to indicate it's Foley."

"Course its Foley," he said. "Got an APB out on him, and told them boys up in north state to get the sonofabitch outta my county. That's what I told Boyle and that's what its goin' be unless you all can come up with something better than this." He tossed the folder on the desk. "Double Eagle boots, injuns..." he mumbled. "You gettin' old, Hank." He leaned back in his chair and clicked a ball point pen in and out. "Thought 'bout early retirement?"

Hank stiffened. He thought about Boyle, and the story the people in Norte del Sur told him about his kid, and he knew that if he said something to Morrison not only would nothing happen, but he'd probably be fired.

He had written a good report on the rash of holdups, but it was obvious Morrison was more interested in covering his ass than solving the crimes.

"Gave it some thought, Sheriff. Lose some of my pension though."

"Sure, sure. Well you think about it Hank. In the meantime, see if you can't catch that Foley bunch."

He tossed the pen onto the folder and rubbed his head. "This thing ain't goin' look good on my record, Hank. I got a shot at state office I do good here. This kinda thing could hurt, and I don't intend takin' the blame. You understand, deputy."

Hank put his hat on his head. "Right you are, Sheriff." He turned and walked out of the office, leaving Morrison rubbing his head. When the door slammed behind the deputy, Morrison took a bottle of pills from his desk and tossed a couple into his mouth.

The man who had been at the Bar Q with the his bleached blonde wife filled the small screen of the TV that balanced on a shelf above the counter of Daisy's Diner.

"I knew they wasn't for real...what I mean is, they was for real," the man said into the Channel 3 microphone. *"What I mean is they was too real to be pretending..."*

"Especially that woman..." the blond interjected. *"Thought for sure she was going to kill poor Mr. Jenkins."*

Hank kept his eyes glued to the screen as he sipped on a cup of coffee. He knew that if he dropped his eyes to the woman standing behind the counter, her elbows set in front of him cushioning her chin, his eyes would invariably be drawn to the large cleavage that her low cut blouse revealed.

"Hope they don't hit my place," Daisy said. "Can't afford no robberies."

Mr. Jenkins, the Bar Q manager, flashed on the screen:

"It was just horrible," he said in his effected voice, rubbing has hands together. *"I just don't understand how something like this could happen..."*

"Don't you worry, Daisy." Hank said. "I don't think these bandits are going to hit any of the regular folks 'round here."

Daisy put her hand on his. He felt its warmth travel through him to the pit of his stomach. He had always been attracted to Daisy, even had a short affair with her when her husband ran off. But then Tex came on the scene, rolling in with his smooth talk and big truck, and that was the end of it.

"Got the report here which verifies my original suspicion that the Foley gang from North State has been responsible for this rash of crimes." Sheriff Morrison' smug face filled the screen. *"We have an APB out, and I expect to have the perpetrators in custody soon."*

Hank laughed, and then found his eyes staring at Daisy's endowment, and knew that she knew what he was looking at. She smiled.

"More coffee, Hank?"

"A...yeah. Thanks."

She turned her back to him and bent slightly in order to get the steaming pot from the warmer, knowing exactly what she was showing off in her tight jeans.

"Ain't seen Tex since he lost that truck of his."

"Sorry to hear that," Hank said in the most sincere voice he could manage.

She turned around and poured the thick black liquid into the mug. "Just as well," she said. "Weren't no future in him." She looked up and smiled. "Been thinking 'bout closin' up the diner. Getting too much for me alone."

"That would be a shame," Hank said. "Money?"

"Naw, just lonely I guess. Well, yes, that too, but I could manage. What I need is someone to share it with I guess." She turned away again and busied herself at the cutting board.

"Been thinking about retiring from the department," Hank said, staring into the steaming coffee. "Be looking for something to get into. Thinking about opening a small bar or something."

Daisy turned around again. "Really, Hank? You know, I've always wanted to add a bar onto the diner. You know, I guess there'd be some real money in a bar out here. Ain't nothing round for miles, and what with the truckers and all..."

"Haven't made up my mind 'bout retiring yet. Have to take a cut in my pension I retire now." He saw a look of disappointment cross her face, the frown going against her makeup. "But nothing says I can't start making an investment now," he added.

"You really interested," Daisy's smile returned, leaving small lines where the makeup had cracked.

"Don't know why not. Can't think of nobody I'd like better doin' business with."

Daisy leaned across the counter and kissed him on the cheek, and then thrust out her hand. "It's a deal, pard."

Hank took her hand and gently squeezed it.

"You come by after closing," Daisy said, "and we'll work out the details over a drink. All the details…"

Hank smiled to himself as he pulled off the main highway onto the dirt road leading to Norte Del Sur. Things were going good; better than he expected. He took a gamble when he convinced his friend in the Motor Vehicle Department to pull Tex's Arizona license. He didn't know if the big Texas trucker would stop seeing Daisy, but as it turned out his hunch was right, and now things were going better than he had planned.

It was getting on to evening when he pulled up in front of the Pass Time. The sun was still glaring in the western horizon. Sundown would come late, and he had some tracking to do.

He pulled his car in next to two vans; one from the Yuma Bar Supply, and the other Motel and Hotel Supply of the West. Several men were unloading crates from the back of the vans, and eyed him as he stepped out of his car.

"Howdy, Hank." Sid was standing on the porch of the Pass Time supervising the unloading. "What brings you out here?"

"Business must be booming, Sid. Where's all this stuff comin' from?" he said, stepping onto the porch and taking his hat off

"Well, business has picked up, you know, with

these holdups and all people starting to come back to Norte del Sur. Just like the old days."

"You mean you're getting all this stuff on credit, Sid?" Hank took out his handkerchief and mopped his brow.

"Credit?" Sid said. "How 'bout a beer, Hank?"

The deputy fell into the chair on the porch. He looked at his watch. "Five o'clock and still hot as hell. Sure, beer be fine."

"Sarah, bring deputy Hank a beer," Sid shouted through the door, and then turned back to the deputy. "No Hank. This stuff just been coming. Invoice says, 'from a benefactor.' You know what that is, Hank... benefactor?"

"Sure, I know what it means."

"Yeah, I figure it's some historical society or something. You know what I mean; figure old Norte del Sur has some historical importance after all. Too bad it takes more bandits to make folks sit up and take notice."

"Your beer, Deputy Hank," Sarah said, handing the deputy a sparkling new glass mug.

Hank took the mug and looked at it for a moment; an indian chief with the insription *Norte del Sur, Arizona* etched into the glass. "Pretty fancy. No bottles?"

"Got a tapper," Sid said. "It's better that way."

"Yeah." He took a drink and wiped his mouth with the back of his hand. "What you think of all these holdups, Sarah?"

"Don't think nothing, Hank. Ain't it the Foley Gang like the Sheriff been saying on TV?"

Sid laughed.

Hank took another drink. "Yeah, well, can't believe everything you see on TV, Sarah. Me myself, I think its a local bunch. Kids maybe. Seen Waco?"

"What's you want with Waco?" Sarah said, color coming to her face.

"Just wondering if you seen him. Got something for him," Hank smiled.

"Took a family down to Mama Lo's for some Mexican food," Sid said. "Took 'em in the touring car. You know, part of the tour and all...trip to old Mexico."

Sarah frowned. "You finished, Hank?"

"What's all this, Hank?" Luke said, walking onto the porch from inside the Pass Time. "You filed our complaint on Boyle's kid, or what?"

The deputy downed the last drops of beer and handed Sarah back the glass mug. "Yeah, figure it's a local bunch behind these holdups myself. But Sheriff Morrison, he thinks it's Foley, and hell, I'm just the deputy," Hank said, trying to ignore Luke.

Sarah took the mug and went back into the Pass Time.

"Well, guess I'll take a ride 'cross the border. See if I can't catch up with Waco."

"What about our complaint?" Luke insisted.

"Never mind that, Luke." Sid said, stepping between the two men. "Things looking better now. No sense looking for trouble. You come back soon, Hank. Thing's changing 'round here. You'll be surprised."

"Yeah, bet I will," Hank said, stepping off the porch and getting back into his car. "You mind and don't let that holdup gang get you, Sid."

"Don't worry 'bout us here. Norte del Sur is the

home of Sheriff Merkins. No bandits come into Norte del Sur. You know, never have and never will."

"Sure thing, Sid. Sure thing." Hank started his engine and sped off down the dirt street toward the border.

"Sign here," one of the delivery men said as Sid watched the deputy's car disappear in a cloud of dust.

"Damnit, Sid. We got to file a charge," Luke said.

"Luke, Mattie's calling you..." Sid said as he took the clipboard from the delivery man.

"Mattie?" Luke rushed back into the Pass Time.

Mama Lo walked into the kitchen, wiping sweat from her face with her apron. Joe and Waco sat at a table with a bottle of tequila between them. Maria was at the stove cooking. Joe had positioned himself so he could admire her.

"These crazy gringos you bring me," the old lady said. "Always they say, we would like to see a menu, and always they order the Special. Maria, four *especials*."

"Hey, their money's good so stop complaining," Waco laughed.

"Who's complaining? I'm no complaining. I just mean these gringos are locos. That's all I'm saying." She went to a long cutting board and started chopping at a hunk of slow roasted pork.

"It no different from when they came through here looking for my Pancho..."

"Okay Mama," Joe laughed. "Only spare us the

history lesson."

"Eh, you *pendejos*. You think you know every-thing," she said, waving the knife in the air, and then slapped it flat side down on the shredded meat when the back door flew open and Jesus ran in panting for air.

"It's the law, man! They coming!"

"Jesus," Maria said, turning from the hot stove. "What's the matter for you?"

"Who's coming?" Waco said, getting up.

"The law, man." Jesus swept past his sister and stopped at the table. "It's Deputy Hank, man. He's talking with Pedro and Señor Cassidy, asking lots of questions 'bout Waco."

Waco and Joe looked at each other.

"Hey, what's going on," Mama Lo said. "You boys ain't in no trouble?"

Waco took her by the arm. "Mama, you go in and tell those folks about Poncho Villa. It's part of the tour." He led her to the door and coaxed her through.

"What do you think?" he said, turning back to Joe. Maria put her hands protectively on Joe's shoulders.

"Hey, he probably just wants to talk. He don't have nothing on us," Joe said.

"Besides," Maria said. "He no have jurisdiction this side of the border."

They both looked at Maria. Joe kissed her hand.

"She's right," he said. "He had anything on us he wouldn't be looking for us here."

"Well, best go see what he wants," Waco started walking to the rear door. "You guys may's well stay here. It's me he's looking for."

The afternoon sun hit Waco with a blinding flash. He took a pair of sunglasses from his pocket and slipped them on as he walked around the adobe building to the front just as the Deputy's car pulled up alongside the touring car. Several people stood outside the other adobe buildings on the dirt street, watching from a distance and wondering what the Arizona cop was doing in Mexico.

"Waco," Hank said, slamming the car door and putting on his hat. "Been looking for you."

"Heard, Hank. What can I do for you?"

Hank put his hand on Waco's shoulder. "Mind we step out of this heat, son." He led Waco toward the covered porch in front of Mama Lo's.

Waco stopped and faced Hank, easing the deputy's hand from him. "What's so important you come down here into Mexico looking for me?"

Hank smiled and wiped his face with his handkerchief. "Damned hot. Seems its hotter this side of the border. Don't know why. Seem like that to you, son?"

"Nope, Hank. Seems cooler to me."

"Well, seems hotter to me."

"Come on Hank, you didn't come here to jabber 'bout the weather. You want me for something?" Waco leaned back against the cool adobe wall.

"Yeah, guess I do Waco. You know, I been knowing you since you was a baby. Knew your ma, grandma and grandpa too. Still see your ma now and again."

"Get to the point Hank. It's too hot to be beating 'round the bush. 'Sides, I got a tour group inside eating lunch, and I got to get back to 'em before they mistake Mama's salsa for ketchup."

"Business been pretty good since these here hold-ups," Hank said. "Might say they saved old Norte del Sur."

"Might say that. Hank." Waco unconsciously rubbed his shoulders on the adobe wall. "Can't say it hurt none."

"You know, I been heading up the investigation on these cases?"

"Thought it was the Foleys. That's what the papers been saying."

Hank put his hands on Waco's shoulders. "Come on Waco. We know that's a crock," and then he stuck his hands into his gun belt and looked away. "No, I figure it's a local bunch. From what I hear sounds like youngsters." He turned back to Waco. "Smart, I grant you, but surely not Foley. Not his style."

"So Hank, what you gettin' at?"

"Ain't getting at nothing, Waco. Just saying it ain't the Foleys. Jesus it's hot." He took off his hat and wiped the lining with his handkerchief. "I figure this gang, they ain't really outlaws at all. Just some locals figure robbing's the only way to get things done. Figure the law ain't fair to poor folks all the time, and they're just playing at being Robin Hood...rob from the rich and give to the poor, like that."

"You figure that do you," Waco said, feeling the sweat rolling down his face. "Well, I don't know nothing about it."

"Sure you don't, son. Sure. Didn't say you did. Have I ever tell you about your grandpa, old Sheriff Merkins? No guess I didn't. Well I'm going to tell you."

Waco wiped the sweat from his face with the back

of his hand, and then wiped his hand on his jeans.

"Well," Hank said. "Old Sheriff Merkins—your grandpa—had a philosophy 'bout law enforcement what kept his town peaceful. You see, back in them days lots of folks was poor, and lots of the outlaws round these parts, well, they was just poor folks robbing from the rich. Kinda equalizing out the wealth in the territory, if you know what I mean. Sheriff Merkins, well he believed the world wasn't a just place and that those that owned everything made the laws to protect themselves. So the Sheriff, he adopted his own sense of justice - kind of a Southern Arizona justice. You know what I'm talking about?"

Waco nodded, still unsure what the deputy was getting at.

"Ole Lemuel, well, he made it clear to all them fellas back then that if they kept their business out of Norte del Sur, he'd keep out of their business. Long as they didn't do nothing to hurt the plain folk in the county, Sheriff Merkins turned his head. Cross him though, and he...well, didn't nobody ever stand trial in Norte del Sur." Hank stepped off the porch back into the sun. "Anyway Waco, I brought you something I thought you could use." He pulled a large box from the front seat of his car.

"You brought me something?" Waco said, stepping off the porch behind the deputy, suspicious of the deputy's sudden generosity.

Hank handed the box to him. "Yeah, couldn't help but notice those Double Eagle boots of yours was getting kinda worn out. Don't many folks wear them Double Eagles no more."

Waco looked down at his boots, and then opened the box. It was a new pair of Mason leather cowboy boots.

"You can tell those Double Eagles by the emblem on the heels. Leaves a clear imprint in the dirt." Hank smiled and slid behind the wheel of the car. "You mind and throw those old boots away, Waco." He fired up the engine, took his hat off and slowly pulled away from Mama Lo's, heading back toward the border crossing.

"He's on to us," Waco said calmly as he walked back into the kitchen and straddling the chair at the small table. Joe remained expressionless.

"How you know this?" Maria said, again moving from the stove to stand behind Joe, wrapping her arms protectively around his neck. "Why he come down here to tell you this?"

"Can't figure it," Waco said, pouring a small glass of tequila. "But he knows, that's sure."

"They come for us we go into the hills," Jesus said. "We shoot them they come for us, just like Pancho."

"Shut up *niño*," Maria snapped. "This ain't TV."

Waco sipped thoughtfully at the tequila. Joe reached up and softly stroked Maria's' arm. "We'd better cool it for awhile," he said. "Think I'll stay put down here for a while." He looked up and smiled at Maria. "If I got a place to stay..."

She kissed him on the top of his head.

Waco smiled. "Better keep Jesus out of sight too."

"Eh, I'm not scared..." the boy protested.

"*Cayate niño*," Maria scolded. "Waco say you stay

down here."

"What about you and Sarah?" Joe said.

"Don't worry 'bout us. We'll be okay. I got a feeling Deputy Hank's on our side. 'Sides, we got a lot of work around the Pass Time. The stuff we ordered been arriving..." he said, pulling off his old boots. "Here Jesus, bury these somewhere."

"*Locos gringos...*" Mama Lo banged into the kitchen. "Now they no want the Special. They want hamburgers. *Locos!* Come all the way to Mexico and they order *hamburquesa* like this is some kind of Burger King or something. *Locos gringos!*"

Chapter Eighteen

"You no listen you end up in the klink sure."
                                        -Old Chief

The ambulance rolled through the blackness of the desert night on a road known to few people—Bandido road they called it. The high pitched drone of a thousand cicadas filled the hot air, drowning out the engine as it pushed the four wheel drive over the ruts of the path. An occasional jack rabbit scampered in front of the headlights, stared for a second, and then disappeared into the darkness. Sidewinders would slither away at the last second, out from the path of the ambulance wheels..

Joe didn't know why he had left the safety and comfort of the border town to set out toward the reservation and his grandfather, the Old Chief. The few days he had shared Maria's bed had been like heaven. He had known women before—white girls, Indian girls—but they had always been one nighters after hooking up at some bar after a night of drinking and dancing. But he always woke up the next morning feeling sad and alone. Maria was different. The fact that she had been a prostitute didn't bother him; in fact, it made her a talented and generous lover. He couldn't explain what it was that made him fall in love with her, but he had. There had always been attracted toher, but he knew she was Waco's friend.

With her he felt complete and happy, and it had been a struggle to leave her. But something inside called out to his spirt, like his ancestors were beckoning him. He knew he had to go.

The World War II ambulance bumped along the all but forgotten cattle path that ran across the border. He knew it all like the back of his hand; the barely visible dirt road that wound through the low foot hills, coming out about a quarter of a mile behind the now abandoned Norte del Sur train station where thousands of head of cattle were once loaded from ranches north and south of the border, bound for the markets in Kansas City, while offering the marauding troops of Pancho Villa a steady supply of beef, and easy pickings for Indians and local rustlers.

From there it was a a straight shot past the Norte del Sur cemetery and on to the Four Feathers road to the reservation. For the untrained eye it was just so much desert and scrub, but Joe knew every inch of it.

Soon he saw a flickering light in the darkness. As the ambulance drew closer he saw a fire burning, casting a long shadow of his grandfather's cabin across the desert. Then he saw the old man, sitting in front of the fire, staring into the flames. A dim blue light lit up the open door of the windowless cabin, and a humming noise, much like the cicadas, floated out into the night air .

Joe stopped a few yards away, got out of the ambulance and slowly approached the fire. The Old Chief didn't look up or acknowledge his presence. He peeked into the cabin where the small black and white television sat with a blank screen, casting the blue light that lit up the room and spilled out into the darkness.

"Something wrong with the TV, Grandpa?" he said, crouching down next to the Old Chief.

The old man continued staring into the flames. "Evil spirit enter TV, sent by Great Spirit of ancestors. 'Too much bull,' Great Spirit tells to me. 'TV too much bull.' Great Spirit talk to me in flames of fire. He tell me many things."

Joe remained silent and stared into the fire, his eyes drawn to the jumping flames and the golden sparks that drifted up into the black desert sky.

"They tell me, 'take to war path against rich white eyes. They tell me young braves become warriors as they seek justice." The Old Chief spoke in monotone as if in a trance, his eyes never leaving the dancing flames. "The Great Spirit says that there will come among you a young warrior who will seek the path of righteousness, and that his deeds will make him Chief of our people..."

The Old Chief lifted his eyes from the fire and looked at Joe. He put his hand on the boy's shoulder. "If that warrior doesn't end up in the Yuma City calaboose."

"Grandpa, what are you talking about?" Joe said.

"Come on, boy. Don't give me no bull. You think age has taken my sight. You and Waco watch too much John Wayne movies. I tell you they all bull. You no listen you end up in the klink sure."

"So what are you saying. Grandpa?," Joe said.

The old man stared back into the flames. "I say you are the one, Joe. You are the chosen one by the Great Spirit to lead our people. For many years I believe it was your brother, but now I know the truth. So, my son, I tell you this and you take it from the many moons this old man has lived under the White Man. You done good, you and Waco. Now is time to cool it."

The Old Chief fell silent, leaving the sound of the crackling fire which he stirred with a stick, sending clouds of sparks dancing and snapping into the still darkness, and ever time the Old Chief stirred the fire Joe would look into the sparkling cloud, and soon an image appeared.

He saw a young Indian brave on a horse with a rifle resting in his lap, looking out over a broad expanse of desert. And he recognized his grandfather, a young brave proudly surveying his domain.

The Old Chief began chanting in a low voice, and Joe suddenly wished he had learned the language of his people better than he had.

His Grandpa was one of the last warriors to remember fighting the white man, and now Joe was fighting the white man. And where he had felt he had joined up with Waco because there was nothing better to do, or because he simply wanted to strike out, suddenly it took on meaning for him. He thought of the picture of his brother with the fat white woman and the new car and tract house. He thought of his friends, many of them dead from fights, liquor or drugs; he thought of his parents, long since lost in the cities of the whites. Was he the last Indian warrior? And then he thought of Sarah and Waco and Maria; Sid, Luke and Mattie, Suzie and Bertha and Mama Lo and Jesus —the people of Norte del Sur—and he knew they were all Apaches; displaced persons in a land with little room or sympathy for them.

And then he remembered the words of the Black social worker who had come to the reservation and had said how his people had once been slaves in America but were freed, but the Indian had been free in America and then made slaves, and that being free or slave made little difference without power, and that their job was to find where their power was.

He walked back to the ambulance and took out a blanket. A coyote howled in the dark. He would sleep under the sky that night and think of his ancestors who had fought for their dignity and their land.

Chapter Nineteen

*"Nothing survives in the desert
without water"*

-Deputy Hank

Hank held his hand over his mouth concealing his pleasure at Sheriff Morrison's discomfort as Representative Rowdy Boyle paced up and down in front of him shouting. The Sheriff nervously punched his ball point pen in and out as sweat poured off his fat face despite the air conditioner hummed loudly forcing cold air into the stuffy office.

The veins stood out from Boyle's neck as he waved a sheet of officious looking paper in Morrison's face.

"It says they found Foley alright; found him in his

hideout up in north state and he's been dead for at least three weeks."

"Listen Rowdy," Morrison said, leaning across his desk. "It must have been Foley's gang. Maybe they're operating without the old man. "

"Bull crap," Boyle shouted. "They picked up Foley's partner in Denver in a flop house. Deputy there said he's been drunk for at least two weeks."

"Well Christ, Rowdy..."

"Morrison, you've got some explaining to do."

The Sheriff's chair let out a moan as he leaned back and started punching the ball point pen in and out again, staring at the little silver ball as it appeared and disappeared.

"I seen your deputy's report on these cases, no thanks to you, and I'm convinced that this is a local job."

Hank stepped forward. "Excuse me, sir, but I don't think these people are local..."

"That's okay, deputy," Boyle said, waving Hank off without taking his eyes from of the Sheriff. "I'm telling you this has got something to do with those people over in Norte del Sur. I'm convinced of it. Those damned people never forgave me for stopping that ghost town from becoming a historic landmark." He was ranting, talking more to himself than the other two men in the office. "Humiliating me in the press, and in front of... and then robbing..." his voice rose again to a high pitch, and he again focused his anger at Morrison. "Robbing the Bar Q in broad day light. Do you realize Morrison that I own 25 percent of the Bar Q, along with some other important people in this state. I'm telling you those people are out to get back at me. But I'm going to fix them." He started mumbling again, as if thinking out loud. "I'll make sure that damn Norte del Sur dries up and blows away. That's what I'll do."

"I'm sorry, sir," the Sheriff said. "I don't follow you. We have no evidence implicating the people in Norte del Sur, except that the holdups have taken place in that vicinity."

"Look here, Morrison, if you can't handle this case I sure and hell will find someone who can. We're going to need extra help on this thing and I want you to deputize some people to assist in the investigation."

Morrison sat forward in his chair again. It squeaked under his weight. "What do you mean? I'm Sheriff here and I'll..."

"Sure, you're Sheriff," Boyle said, "only because I made you sheriff, and don't you forget it."

He opened the door and called in a group of teen-age boys wearing Arizona State University sweat shirts. Hank recognized the boy in front from the picture in the newspaper. It was Boyle's son, Butch, the same one the people at Norte del Sur accused of breaking up the Pass Time.

"These kids got sand wagons..."

"Dune buggies, dad," his son corrected.

"Whatever," Boyle said. "They can patrol the desert since your people can't seem to get off the main high-way."

Morrison's s face was now bright red and swet dripped down his nose. He pulled out a wrinkled handkerchief and mopped it. "'Now listen, I can't do that..."he started to protest.

"Sure you can," Boyle said, leaning across the desk. "You're the Sheriff. What do you say, deputy." He turned his head back to Hank who shrugged his shoulders, and then sat in the chair in front of Morrison and smiled. "And if you want to ever be anything more than Sheriff, I think you'll cooperate with me. You get my drift, Morrison."

"Excuse me. Sheriff," Hank said, stepping between the group of boys. I got some things to do."

"Sure Hudnel. You take care of your duties." Morrison said, dismissing the deputy with another wave of his hand.

Hank started to walk out. "And Hudnel..."

He turned around.

"Get over to Norte del Sur and see what you can find out."

Hank put his hat on his head and walked out of the office. He heard Morrison's voice drift out over the roar of the air conditioner.

"Raise your right hands and repeat after me...."

The heat in the diner was oppressive even though Daisy had three fans going and the door wide open. Hank stared into a cup of coffee, wondering why he had asked for it. Daisy leaned across the counter and ran her hand through his steel gray hair. She had a sixth sense about people, telling anyone who would listen how working in a diner for so many years and observing people had given her this special insight.

Hank's eyes drifted up to her blouse that was opened one button more than usual. Droplets of sweat rolled down from her neck, leaving paths through her heavy pancake makeup, and slid down between her large bosom.

"Should I put out the closed sign?" she whispered.

Hank stared back into the coffee cup. "You know," he said after a moment's silence. "Every time I came to eat lunch here and saw that rig outside and the closed sign in the window, I wished it was me in here and not that braggart Texan." He looked at Daisy. Her eyes said she didn't understand; her "sixth sense" failed. "Now, well beautiful, now that it's me, it's too damned hot and I'm too damned depressed."

"I'm sorry baby, is there anything mama can do?" Daisy said. Disappointment was no stranger to her.

"It ain't right, Daisy. There's something screwed up. How come it's always the good folks in this world that get the shaft."

"I don't understand, Hank. What are you trying to say?"

"Well, look at you, for instance," Hank said. "You're a good woman. Never hurt nobody. And yet, every time you trust somebody you get hurt."

Daisy pulled away from him, but he caught her hand and squeezed it.

"Until now. But Daisy, look how long it took."

She smiled again and pressed his hand to her breast.

"I'm sorry honey, but..."

"It's okay, I understand," He leaned across the counter and kissed her on the lips. "I got to get going."

"You coming back this evening. Hank? We got to

work out the details about the bar," she smiled coyly.

"Yup, I'll be here, but let's not waste time talking," he winked.

"You nasty old man," she laughed as he put his hat back on his head and walked to the door. "Bring a bottle of bourbon like a good boy," she shouted after him as he walked back into the blinding sun.

Driving down the highway toward the Norte del Sur turnoff Hank wondered what he was going to do, or if there was anything he could do. He was counting on the new fame of the small town to make a bar at Daisy's a workable investment for his retirement. He had daydreamed about setting up an old western saloon and making a fortune with Daisy at his side. The thought took a lot of sting out of his not being made sheriff, but it had all hinged on the success of Norte del Sur, and now Rowdy Boyle, owner of the Southern Arizona Fresh Spring Water Company, was going to ruin his plans. Nothing could survive in the desert without water, and he knew that was what Boyle was planning.

He pulled off the main highway at the Norte del Sur turnoff, growing more depressed at the prospect of telling the old folks about Boyle and his plans to shut off their water.

His car caught up with a bus that was slowly rolling over the dirt road. The bus said *Tours of the Old West - Yuma, Az.* on the back. There was no room to pass, so he had to slow down and follow it into the town, glad that Garrett had insisted on air conditioned cars so he could roll up his windows against the dust being kicked up from the bus tires. When they finally reached the main street the bus slowed more, as if the driver were unsure of where he was going, until it came to the Pass Time and stopped. Hank pulled in next to it. Two cars and a small camper were parked alongside the old touring car. Several children were splashing in a plastic swimming pool in front of the cabin.

Hank opened his door. The heat hit him with a blast and sweat immediately popped from his forehead. He took out his handkerchief and ran it over his face as he approached the bus.

The driver opened the door.

"Howdy Hank. Ain't breaking any speed limits am I," he laughed.

"Max, what brings you out here?"

"Hey, Norte del Sur is the happening thing, man," the small bespectacled man laughed again. The heat had gotten to him as soon as he had opened the bus doors, and the wax in his slicked back black hair was melting down the side of his face. There was a family with two kids and an elderly couple sitting in the bus. "People want to come to Norte del Sur, man. Ever since its been in the papers and on TV. Figured I'd get in early 'fore some touring company figures it out."

Sid came out of the Pass Time and walked up to the bus. "Welcome to Norte del Sur," he said tipping the brim of his large Baily Ford cowboy hat.

"Howdy," the driver said. "Think my people can get a drink of water and a short tour. You know, some history and some souvenirs," he winked.

"Sure, that's what we're here for," Sid said. "Bring

'em in."

Sid slapped Hank on the back. "Brother, we're in business here."

"Sid, I got to talk with you," Hank said.

"Sure, Hank. Just as soon as I get these folks inside and get them whatever they want. Bet you could do with a glass of water or lemonade yourself."

Hank mopped his face with the handkerchief again. "Sure Sid. Could do with a glass of water." He put his arm around Sid's bony shoulder. "Sure looks like you're going to make a killing here."

"You bet, deputy. Just like I always said"

"Say," the driver said, helping his passengers down from the bus. "When you going to get a paved road into here. Going to be a lot of traffic to Norte del Sur in the future."

Hank took his arm from Sid's shoulder. Suddenly it became impossible for him to say what he had come to say. "I'll take a rain check on that water, Sid. I've got to get back to the highway."

"Sure thing, Hank. You come back real soon." Sid turned to the people getting off the bus. "Welcome to Norte del Sur, the last of the real wild west towns..."

Chapter
Twenty

"...if you no killed someone, and your pistola work, than it must be the woman."

-Old Mexican

The afternoon sun was dipping down into the west in a blaze of red and pink and orange as Waco guided the pinto in the direction the the old Mexican's shake. To outside eyes it would be a mystery how he knew where he was going, riding silently through the open desert like that. But people who live in the desert are guided by their knowledge and instinct as sure as if there were street signs and landmarks to guide them.

He had to get away. He had a burning need inside

him to talk to someone, but there was no one in Norte del Sur, on either side of the border, he could confide in. They would all offer their opinions and advice, and while he knew it was because they cared for him that they would try to make things right for him he just wanted someone to listen, and only the Old Mexican listened to him without judgement, without advise. Just understanding.

By the time he reached the shack the sun had disappeared and the sky had turned a deep purple, revealing the first stars of the evening. A small rooster gave its farewell crow to the day before marching into the shed where the old man kept his horse and goats. Waco dismounted and followed the rooster.

The Old Mexican greeted him at the doorway of his one room adobe shack. "Ahh, me *amigo* Waco. What brings you to my humble home? You on the lam? You kill somebody with your grandpoppa's *pistola.*"

"No, no, nothing like that."

"Bueno. You come at the right time," the old man smiled, holding the door open for Waco. "I just made some stew."

The small room was filled with the aroma of cooking meat and chilies. Waco took off his hat and sat at the small table in the middle of the one room shack as the old man dished up the steaming brown stew from a metal pot, dumped it into a wooden bowl and placed it in front of him along with a basket of warm tortillas. Waco remembered he hadn't eaten all day and his stomach growled in anticipation.

Sweat immediately beaded up on his forehead with the first bite as the chili-fortified stew sent fire into his empty stomach. Waco was accustomed to hot food —Mama Lo's cooking had made sure of that—but this was something altogether different. But as hot as it wasthe flavors of the rich sauce and succulent meat came through. The old man watched with satisfaction as Waco gobbled it down while stuffing hunks of the tortilla into his mouth to absorb the heat.

"You like my little stew. I make this for our *compañeros in* the army," he said.

The old man finished eating, sat back in his chair and stared at Waco. "Maybe you like a little something to drink now," he said.

Waco nodded.

The old man fetched a bottle from his shelf. It had no label on it so Waco figured it was home made. Many of people in the area made their own; more a pulque than tequila, and the kind the Indians of Sonora made was powerful..

Waco hunched over the table, quietly sipping the milky liquid and listening to the hot wind whistling through the open boards of the shack.

"So *chamaco*, what are you doing here in the middle of the desert?" the old man said, breaking the silence.

Waco sat back in the chair. The mescal and food relaxed him. He had felt restless and uneasy since that afternoon at Grandma Poppy's house, when he and Sarah had kissed and he heard her say she loved him. It wasn't that he didn't feel the same way, or that it had made his heart happy to hear her say it, but that ever since that rainy night when he had killed the cow and found Grandma Poppy dead everything had changed.

He had always been comfortable with the way things were; with Norte del Sur and the old folks, and the small border town with Mama Low, Jesus and Maria, and with his childhood pal, Sarah. But now all that had changed, and he wasn't sure if it made him happy or sad.

After a few minutes the old man asked, "It's a woman, no?

"Waco looked up from his glass. "Why do you say that?"

"Well, if you no killed someone, and your *pistola* work, than it must be the woman you talked about last time you were here."

Waco sat quietly for a moment. He had a painful need to tell someone about Sarah, but had no one he felt comfortable confiding in. He poured another shot of mescal and then it all burst out of him. He told the old Mexican about everything that had happened since he had last been there. He explained about Norte del Sur and how he wanted to help the old folks who were like his family, and how Sarah had joined up with them and master minded the Bar Q robbery. And then he told the old man about his feelings for Sarah, and how they had now changed, and his feelings of being inadequate because she was so much smarter than he, and because he didn't know how to make love to her...he fell silent, embarrassed by his admission, and thinking that the old Mexican probably thought less of him because of what he had said.

He looked at the old man expecting ridicule, but only saw a smile, the light of the kerosine lamp shining off his gold teeth, and the look of understanding in his dark eyes.

The old man knew Waco would never believe that he too knew about love, and what it did, and what it meant. Hadn't he been in love with the same woman for over forty years; she who hadn't given him a thought in all that time. He was half tempted to share his secret with Waco; to show the *chamaco* the picture of Mama Lo when her hair flowed down like black silk over her smooth shoulders, and her slender body with young breasts that stood erect under her peasant blouse, with almond shaped black eyes that sparkled over her high cheek bones that were smoothly molded in a deep bronze. How could he tell the young man how his love had been swept away from him when General Villa rode into the small Mexican town called Norte del Sur, and he had taken her up in his arms, ruining her for any other man forever; not that he was more than any man, but that he was Pancho Villa and he was bigger than life itself. And the old man would admit that even losing his woman, Pancho Villa was his leader, and he rode with him for years because he knew he had to fight for what was right, always knowing that the woman he loved was lost to him forever. He understood Waco's pain, but he also knew that there was nothing he could say that could make it okay. Instead he reached behind him and grabbed his guitar that he had carried with him since he rode with the Mexican General, the man who had taken his woman from him. He filled Waco's glass and then his own.

"*Salud, Chamaco.*" he downed the liquor and then slowly began to strum the guitar strings. Then he began to sing. His voice was soft and melodic as the

years seemed to fall off him as he drifted back to his
youth in Pancho Villa's Army.

En lo alto de la abrupta serranía
acampado se encontraba un regimiento
y una moza que valiente los seguía
locamente enamorada del sargento.

Popular entre la tropa era Adelita
la mujer que el sargento idolatraba
que ademas de ser valiente era bonita
que hasta el mismo Coronel la respetaba.

Y se oía, que decía, aquel que tanto la quería:

Y si Adelita se fuera con otro
la seguiría por tierra y por mar
si por mar en un buque de guerra
si por tierra en un tren militar.

Y si Adelita quisiera ser mi esposa
y si Adelita ya fuera mi mujer
le compraría un vestido de seda
para llevarla a bailar al cuartel.

In the heights of a steep mountainous range
a regiment was encamped
and a young woman bravely follows them
madly in love with the sergeant.

Popular among the troop was Adelita
the woman that the sergeant idolized

and besides being brave she was pretty
that even the Colonel respected her.

And it was heard, that he, who loved her so much,
said:

If Adelita would leave with another man
I'd follow her by land and sea
if by sea in a war ship
if by land in a military train.

If Adelita would like to be my wife
If Adelita would be my woman
I'd buy her a silk dress
to take her to the barrack's dance.

Waco's eyes grew heavy as the old man's voice blended with the wind sweeping outside, whistled in through the windows of the shack. He fell into a dreamless sleep.

Chapter
Twenty-one

"She's Indian, "Indians always get mistreated."
                                    -Fran Little Feather

Suzie had a feeling something was going on, but her suspicions weren't confirmed until Sarah shyly agreed to have her hair done. Everyone had always hoped that Sarah and Waco would get together. She had watched the children of her friends leave Norte del Sur until only the children of their children were left, and while she had always tried to keep up appearances for the others, late at night she had feelings of finality—that she and Mattie, Luke and Sid, and Bertha were the end; that the road to Norte del Sur was slowly being swept away on the desert wind, and when they were gone so too would all traces of Norte del Sur. But now that her hopes that there would be someone to take their places she was still troubled.

She looked over at the girl who kept a steady eye on the highway as she guided the old Ford out of Yuma. She was a pretty girl, her bleached blond hair shimmering in the bright sun, reflecting off the newly organized arrangement of curls and carefully placed strands that rolled down her slender neck. Her blue eyes sparkled with the maturity of awakened womanhood.

"Sarah," she said quietly. "I have something to say, and I want you to listen to me this time."

Sarah glanced over at her and smiled, as she always smiled when Suzie got that motherly tone in her voice.

"You're young and there are many paths in front of you." She paused.

"Sure Auntie," Sarah said.

"No, I want you to really listen to me."

"I'm listening Auntie," Sarah insisted.

Suzie knew that it was foolish to expect the girl to heed what she was going to ay, but she had to say it anyway.

"When you're young there are many ways you can go, and God knows these days there are more opportunities open for a young girl than when I was a girl. Some roads you take open to more roads, and some roads lead you down a one way street. Honey, I don't expect you to know what I'm talking about, but I have to tell you and I want you to try to understand."

"Okay Auntie, I'm listening," Sarah said, trying to be patient while keeping her eyes on the highway, and getting a little annoyed.

"I ain't never told any one else this. No one in Norte del Sur knows about my past, not even Sid. Oh, they have a vague idea, but I never told them and they never asked."

'So Auntie, why are you telling me now?"

"Because I think it's important that you should know. Now more than ever."

Sarah looked over at the old woman. "Alright, I'm listening," she said and a pang of sadness struck her.

"My parents were dirt farmers in Oklahoma.," Suzie began. "They were honest folk, but all I could see was being poor and having a lot of babies, and I didn't want that to be my life. So I ran away when I was young. There were few opportunities for a poor country girl like me, and I...well, let's just say I met a man who took me in."

Sadie stopped for a moment, and Sarah saw he dabbing at her eyes with her hanky. Then she cleared her troat and continued.

"I was in love and I really thought he loved me, but I soon found out he had other plans. He talked me into being an entertainer, if you know what I mean."

Sarah looked over at the woman she called Auntie and saw more tears as they slowly rolled down her face, marring her makeup.

"You don't have to explain, auntie. I think I understand. What's important in now..."

"What I'm trying to say, child, is that I love you very much. We all love you; me and your grandma and grandpa, and Sid, and even Bertha, and we want what's best for you and Waco..."

"I love Waco," Sarah said, the words sliding out easier than she thought they would. "And we ain't done nothing we're ashamed of."

Suzie smiled. "Oh honey, I'm sure you haven't done nothin' you'd be ashamed of. Heck, I was...well, never mind, but I was, let us say, experienced by the time I was your age. But things were different back then. The older you get the fewer roads are open to you. I just don't want you to get stuck on a dead end too soon..."

Sarah pulled the wheel of the car, steering it off the main highway onto the dirt road leading to Norte del Sur.

"This is my home, Auntie. You guys are my family. Don't worry about anything." She placed her hand reassuringly on Suzie's without taking her eyes from the road. She knew everyone was afraid she'd run off when she grew up, just like her mother had. "Waco and me, we're going to make sure everything's okay. You'll see."

Suzie fell silent for a moment, and then leaned over and looked at herself in the rearview mirror. "Oh, this darn heat is horrible on my makeup." She fussed with her hair. "Do you think Sid will notice. It's new you know."

The old Ford bounced down the main street of Norte del Sur. Sarah slowed up when she saw a beat up Volkswagen van with colorful cactus flowers painted all over it parked next to one of the deserted buildings. She came to a stop just as a tall man with shoulder length hair came out. He wore dirty blue jeans with a huge Navajo silver belt buckle. His faded flannel shirt was open in front revealing a darkly tanned hairless chest.

"Howdy." The man greeted them with a toothy grin. "Hope it's okay. Looks abandoned."

"Can I help you?" Sarah said.

Suzie turned her head, "I knew it," she muttered". "Damn hippies going to come..."

A woman came out from the building. She wore a full skirt of rough colorful cloth covered by a faded flannel shirt much like the man's. She was adorned with an array of silver and turquoise jewelry. She walked up next to the man and smiled at Sarah.

"Name's Travler," the man said, extending a hand which Sarah accepted. "My wife, Fran Little Feather."

The woman kept smiling at Sarah, and then offered her hand. Sarah took it.

"We come down from New Mexico," the man said. "I work the leather; you know saddles, belts, like that. My woman, she works the silver and turquoise. She's a real artist."

You made these?" Sarah said to the woman. "Auntie, look at this work."

Suzie refused to look.

"Forgive my aunt," Sarah said. "We don't get many strangers here. Not 'til recently anyway. She's kind of behind the times."

The Indian woman moved around to the passenger side of the car. "These are beautiful," she said admiring Suzie's silver earrings. "They're not Navajo..."

Suzie was forced to smile at the flattery. "Why no, they come from Oaxaca as a matter of fact. That was many years ago..."

"They are exquisite," the Indian woman said. "It is rare to see such fine craftsmanship."

"My wife, she's one of the best craftsmen in New Mexico," Travler said. "Trouble is, too much competition on the reservation. Too much commercialism there nowadays. People nowadays don't know the real thing from the cheap imitations everyone's hawking these days. 'Sides, the tribe takes their piece of the action. Been looking for another place to settle and raise a family. Little Feather's expecting a smaller feather."

He laughed at his joke. Sarah smiled politely, but Suzie saw no humor in the man's levity.

"Expecting?" she said. "You got no business out in this hot sun, child. You get yourself right down to the Pass Time and we'll get you a glass of lemonade and in the shade. I can see that no good man of yours got no sense. None of them do when it comes to babies. You get in this car and we'll take you ..."

Sarah looked at the man and shrugged her shoulders as Suzie swung open the door of the car and coaxed the woman in. "And you can come too," she said to Travler.

"You folks looking to settle down, this is the right place," Suzie said with motherly authority to the Indian woman. "Norte de Sur is coming alive. Young man," she shouted out the window. "You follow us down to the Pass Time. Sid will take care of the business of getting you in. Sarah, drive."

"Welcome to Norte del Sur," she said to Travler, and then stepped on the throttle of the Ford.

The man stared at the cloud of dust as the car rolled down the street. He laughed, "Damn, if we ain't found a home."

* * *

Sid climbed down from the water tower as the Ford pulled up between the two station wagons that were parked in front of the Pass Time, and watched as the three women got out. Suzie smiled at him and puffed up her hair.

"Hi handsome," she said coyly. "Got some folks interested in settling in our town. This one..." She turned to the woman.

"Fran," the woman said. "Fran Little feather."

"She's expecting," Suzie said, not noticing the worried look on Sid's face.

Sid's expression was not lost on Sarah. "Auntie, why don't you take Fran inside. We'll be along."

Suzie whispered into Sarah's ear. "He didn't notice my hair. You think he doesn't like it?"

"I'm sure he likes it, Auntie. You take Fran inside."

Suzie winked at Sid. "Things getting better around here, honey."

Sarah waited until Suzie and the Indian woman went into the Pass Time.

"What's wrong, Sid?"

He looked up at the water tower. "Water's low," he said. "Getting down there fast with all these folks comin' 'round. Not that I'm complaining, but you know what I mean."

"So, we'll just have to get a tanker in here from Yuma. Way things are going, we're going to need lots of water," Sarah said.

What she didn't see was the letter from the The Southern Arizona Water Company sticking out of Sid's pants pocket saying they would no longer service the

Norte del Sur area. Sid hadn't told anyone about it.

"Sure," he said. "Tell Suzie I'm taking the car. Got some business in Yuma."

He went to the Ford and got in.

Sarah followed him. "Uncle Sid, nothing's wrong, is there?"

"Naw," he said, sticking his head out of the window and looking into the clear blue of the desert sky where a couple of vultures slowly circled, their bodies black against the white sun. "Something's dying in the desert," he said and then started the engine. He jammed the floor shift, grinding the gears into reverse. Sarah watched as he sped down the main street swerving around the old VW van coming toward the Pass Time.

She turned and walked into the Pass Time with out waiting for Travler to get out of the van. The warm breeze from the new overhead fans ruffled her fresh curls. The large screen color TV cast a flickering light from the dark corner where Mattie and Bertha were sitting in large easy chairs. Luke leaned across the bar, resting his head on his elbows, listening as Suzie exhorted the benefits of moving to Norte del Sur to the Indian woman.

"Sid went into Yuma," Sarah said as she came up to the bar.

Suzie went silent, puffing up her new hairdo again. "Yuma?" she said.

 "Why'd he go into Yuma?" Luke asked.

"Don't know. Didn't say." Sarah sat at one of the stools. "Anyone seen Waco?"

He didn't mention my new hairdo?" Suzie said.

 "Why don't you just tell him your stuck on him?"

Luke scolded.

Suzie looked away, then turned back looking Luke in the eyes. "It wouldn't be lady like."

"Anybody seen Waco?" Sarah repeated.

"No, can't say I have," Luke said.

Suddenly, for no reason, Bertha got up from her chair and walked over to the Indian woman. Without saying a word she took the woman's necklaces gentle in her hands and seemed to be inspecting them. The woman looked over at Sarah who gave her a reassuring nod.

"Fine craftsmanship," Bertha said, more to herself then anyone else. "Good quality stone. Navajo. Yes, definitely Navajo."

Suzie gentle took Bertha's hands from the necklaces. "This is Bertha," she said to the woman.

Bertha looked up at Suzie. "You see," she said. "This girl is Navajo. A very proud people..." she wandered back to her chair and sat down, staring back into the TV.

"What's with her?" It was Travler. He had just come into the room, wiping the sweat from his face with the dirty bandana.

"Sit down," Luke said. "If you folks are interested in moving to Norte del Sur, you may as well get to know us."

He drew a couple of glasses of beer from the new Bud tap, and brought them to the table. "Bertha's had a tough go of it. She's Yaqui you see. Well, back during the Mexican Revolution - that's a while back - she took up with this officer in General Carranza's Army. She must have been no more than a kid then." Luke sat down at the table, getting involved in his own story. "For one reason or another, this officer, he got into some trouble, and he came across the border, bringing Bertha with him. Then he dropped her here in Norte del Sur. Well, Sheriff Merkins and his wife Poppy— we just buried her—looked after her for awhile, but she kept running off with this guy or that guy. But she always came back here, like it was her home, and she's always been like family around here..." his voice trailed off.

"She's Indian," Fran Little Feather said holding the small swelling of her belly. "Indians always get mistreated."

"Well, not here," Suzie said. "And you folks are welcome to move in, ain't that right Luke."

"Sure thing, right Sarah?" he turned back to where Sarah was sipping on a glass of water at the bar.

"Huh," she said. She always turned off when the old folks started telling stories. She'd heard them all a million times. Besides, she was concerned about Sid, and even more, worried about Waco.

"Said they was welcome." Luke shouted.

"Sure, grandpa. You're the boss."

"I'm kinda honorary mayor," he said proudly to the new comers. "Me and Sid, we kind of share running this place, but truth be know, Suzie here's the boss."

Suzie blushed and they all laughed.

"So, we can rent one of them places down there?" the Indian woman said.

"I spotted a good place," Travler said. "Room for a work shop, and a living space."

"Bet he's talking 'bout old man Tailor's store, Luke,"

Suzie said.   '

"Good place. Young fella like you fix it up in no time. Don't worry 'bout rent. We'll discuss that with Sid when he gets back from Yuma. You folks get settled."

Travler jumped up from his chair. "Man, this is great." He tugged at the woman, pulling her from her chair. "Come on honey, let's get started."

"Just one thing," Luke said "Can't sell no Indian blankets or pottery. We gave that concession to someone else."

"No problem," Travler said, hurrying his wife toward the door.

The Indian woman broke from his grip and walked over to Bertha. She took a necklace from her neck and placed it around Bertha's, whispering something into her ear. Then she rejoined Travler and they went through the door, letting a blast of hot air rush into the room.

Bertha got up from her chair and went over to the mirror behind the bar. She caressed the necklace and smiled.

Chapter Twenty-two

"Maria's gone back to San Luis and
you're sitting here!"
                                        -Sarah

The sun finally set over Norte del Sur, dropping the temperature to a relatively comfortable 80 degrees. Luke had gotten the new comers situated in a vacant cabin, the one with a kitchenette, as it would be a few days before they would get old man Tailor's place livable. Suzie sat in the corner with Mattie and Bertha rambling on about how new life was coming to Norte del Sur, her voice being swallowed up by a "Bonanza" rerun. It seemed as if she had stopped worrying about Sid, but Sarah knew how Suzie would talk on and on when she was worried. She, on the other hand, became very quiet when she was worried, and at that moment she was sitting alone in the corner of the bar, away from everyone.

Where was he she wondered. Was he angry because they hadn't made love—gone all the way? But then, it wasn't her that stopped anything from happening. Secretly she had hoped he wouldn't stop; she wanted him even though she didn't know what exactly it was she wanted, or what it would be like; only that a longing had consumed her at that moment, overcoming all thought, and that her body ached with desire. She always thought he was "experienced." She was convinced that he and Maria—how could he be close friends with her and not have gone all the way? Just the thought that they had never made love lessened her dislike for the Mexican girl. And when she had seen those boys try to force themselves on her—when Joe had taken a beating for his heroic rescue—she had second thoughts and felt ashamed at how she had treated the girl in the past.

Suddenly the door slammed open, jarring her from her thoughts, and there stood the Old Chief in full regalia; headdress of feathers flowing down to his legs, leather leggings and war paint smeared carelessly over his face so he looked fearsome in a clownish way.

"Luke, my partner in business," the old Chief shouted. "A Bud if you would."

It was late by the time Waco tied up his horse to the hitching post that had survived years of cars bumping into it. He fumbled with the reins. His head was filled with troubling thoughts since leaving the Old Mexican's.

He had gone back to Mama Lo's looking for Joe.

Besides still being a little drunk he felt a sense of relief after talking with the Old Mexican. It hadn't changed anything, but he felt a weight lifted from his shoulders. But when he got across the border, Jesus ran to him, telling him how Joe had left without a word, and Maria, after crying for hours, had gone to the mirror, made herself up, put on her tight skirt and low cut blouse, and left. Jesus knew where she had gone, and Waco suddenly felt an urgency to see Sarah. She had become more important to him than anything else, and now his desire to find her left him feeling guilty because he hadn't gone to find Joe, and he hadn't rushed off to San Luis to get Maria.

Waco saw the ambulance parked carelessly in front of the Pass Time. Maybe it was Joe, but he never parked like that.

He walked through the open door and was met by Sarah's eyes.

"Where the hell have you been? I've...we've been worried sick," she scolded.

He walked to the bar and sat next to her, nodding to Luke and the Old Chief. The late movie was lighting up the corner where the Mattie and Bertha were both asleep on the new sofa.

"How come you're here chief?" he said? "Thought you said you'd never enter a white man's house?"

The Old Chief laughed and but his hand on Luke's shoulder. "No, I said I'd never come here because beer no good." His hand slipped to the Budweiser tap. "Now my good friends have good beer. Bud, easy to say, easy to pour, easy to drink." He took a long swallow from the glass in front of him.

"Yeah," Luke added. "The Chief and Sid made a deal; he gets exclusive rights to sell Indian blankets and pottery, and he's going to bring down a group from the reservation twice a week to put on a dance for the tourists."

"Once a week," the Old Chief corrected. "I said once a week, and they get free beer."

"Right, if that's what Sid said. But no beer until after the show."

"Okay," the Chief said.

"Where's Joe?" Waco managed to get in.

"Joe, him in desert talking with ancestors. Him going to be chief."

"How's about a beer, Waco," Luke said, pouring from the tap. This stuff's great, better than that bottled stuff we used to stock."

"What's going on?" Sarah whispered, holding his arm. "Where the hell you been?"

Waco stared into the glass of golden liquid, concentrating on the small bubbles floating to the top of the glass. "Damn, I wish Joe was here, Sar. Joe ought to be here."

"Why? Tell me what's happening."

"I wish I knew. Joe disappeared from Maria's without a word, and now Jesus tell's me she's gone back to San Luis. Joe 'ought to be here." He took up the glass and drained it in one drink.

"What!" Sarah said, letting her voice rise. "Maria's gone back to San Luis and you're sitting here!"

Luke and the Old Chief looked over at them. Waco kept his eyes staring at the empty glass.

"So, what am I suppose to do? I wanted to see

you..."

"Waco!" She was nearly shouting. "Maria's your friend. We have to stop her. Damnit, Waco. How could you?" She jumped off the stool and grabbed him by the arm. "We've got to get her."

"Go to San Luis?" Waco stammered. "It's late at night."

"Yes!" She pulled him from the stool. "Damn, Sid took the car. Chief, we've got to take the ambulance. It's for Joe."

The Old Chief dropped off his stool. He was a little unsteady from drinking beer all night. "Maria? Joe's Maria he tells me of. You take the ambulance. I find Joe."

"You can take my horse," Waco said. She's in front."

Sarah grabbed the ambulance keys from the Old Chief and then pulled Waco out of the Pass Time. "I'll drive. It's obvious you're in no condition..."

Chapter Twenty-three

"I believe the lady said she didn't care for your company."

-Waco

It was five in the morning by the time Maria walked into the La Belle Cantina. She had called her cousin who drove a taxi in San Luis, and it took him three hours to drive the brightly painted 1950 Chevy over the washed out road to the Norte del Sur border crossing. It would have been shorter if the taxi went across the border, and crossed back at Norte del Sur, but the *migra* was cracking down on border crossings by Mexican citizens.

As she rode in the car, watching the big fluffy dice dangling from the rear view mirror bounce up and down, she kept seeing Mama Lo and the sadness on her face when she saw that Maria was going back to her old life in San Louis. She could feel the tears that dripped down the old woman's fat face as if they were her own. She had said nothing, but Maria knew what she was thinking; about how pleased she had been when Maria had come to her and announced that she was quitting and could she work at the restaurant. And she knew that Mama Lo highly approved of her and Joe being together. But it was all just a stupid dream. Joe was just using her; a place to hang out until things cooled down. She always believed he had despised her for what she was, what she had to be to support herself and her brother. It was stupid to think he could love her, understand or care. No one cared but Waco; sweet Waco who never asked for anything but friendship.

The engine of the ambulance howled like a dying cat and then stopped altogether.

"Damnit," Sarah said. "The Chef left the head-lights on and the battery 's dead. "Waco..."

She looked over where Waco was sound asleep in the passenger seat. She couldn't help but smile. She couldn't bring herself to be angry with him. She kissed him on the cheek and e went back into the Pass Time.

Luckily Luke had a charger in the back of his tool shed, but it would take hours to recharge enough to get it started. Luke hooked up the cables and Sarah returned to the Pass Time with him, leaving Waco asleep in the ambulance.

The few girls still hanging around the bar in the La Belle paid no attention to her entrance. Juan, the fat owner, didn't say a word; he cared little that she had been gone. All that concerned him was that he got his cut. One girl more or less made no difference to him. There were always plenty of poor girls in Northern Mexico with no where to turn for money.

She suddenly felt hungry, and ordered some eggs and a beer. The sky was turning gray as dawn approached, and there was bound to be some drunk gringos coming in looking for a good time, or some lonely Mexican on his way to work.

As Maria picked at the large platter of scrambled eggs and chirizo a stream of sunlight flowed through the door like a spotlight, illuminating the dust that floated heavily in the air and revealing the grime that was usually hidden in a dull glow of red neon lights. The morning heat seemed to increase the sour smell of stale beer and urine that permeated the place.

Trucks started rolling on the streets outside as the border town came to life. All of a sudden she was sick to her stomach as a feeling of disgust ran through her; disgust with herself, the cantina, and the way of life she had vowed to give up.

The roar of what sounded like motorcycles broke the

quiet, and Chiquita, one of the bar girls rushed inside, holding her tight skirt up so her short legs could move freely.

"American college boys," she loudly whispered as she came up to the bar where the other girls gathered around her like a flock of chickens. "Four of them..." she said breathlessly, pulling a pocket compact from her waist band and fixing her makeup.

The other girls started preening themselves for the perspective customers; all but Maria who turned her back to the bar to face the door.

In they came, four hulking young men with Arizona State U. sweatshirts and tight jeans, swaggering as they walked up to the bar, glancing at the line of women and joking among themselves. Maria recognized them right away, especially the one who was the loudest and obviously the leader. They demanded beer as several of the girls drifted over to them, squeezing between the young men and pressing their bodies against them seductively.

"How about a drink, handsome..." the standard line. Maria stayed at her place, staring at the one who had attacked her at Norte del Sur until he glanced over and she saw the recognition in his face.

"You," he said loudly. "I know you."

Maria continued staring at him. He pushed back the girl next to him and walked over to her. "I seen you somewhere before."

"*Cabron*." she said. "You seen me before, you and your *pinche* pals. Norte del Sur." She spit the words out, her eyes flashing with hatred.

He stood for a moment with a blank expression, and

then a smile slowly crossed his face. "Norte del Sur," he said, and turned back to his friends and laughed. "Sure, you guys remember. That piece of shit town we busted up." He turned back to her. "And you're that little hot tamale. Where's that injun buddy of yours? I still got business with that punk." He moved closer to her. "But first I think I'll finish my business with you."

Waco opened his eyes as the sun was rising in the east, casting its red heat across the desert like a raging wild fire.

"Looks like another hot one," he said. "Where are we?"

"We're coming into Yuma," Sarah answered. "You've been sleeping for hours." Her anger at him had faded, replaced by worry that they would be too late; that Maria would have done something she would regret. She had no idea what had driven Maria back to San Luis, but whatever it was couldn't be important enough for her to go back to a life she now detested.

Waco sat up and rubbed his sore neck. *What are we doing in Yuma?" Oh yes. Maria,* he reminded himself as his aching brain came awake. *I wonder if the Old Chef found Joe. Joe should be here.*

They pulled up to the border crossing. The Mexican guard looked them over suspiciously.

"Why you entering Mexico so early, *jovenes?*

Sarah looked at him. "That's not your business," she said.

"I'm making it my business, *Señorita.* you are the

second group of young *gringos* entering Mexico this morning."

Waco leaned across Sarah. *"Perdónela por favor. Ella es un poco tímida. Queremos casarnos, en seguida."*

The guard smiled and gave Waco a wink. *¿"Aquellos otros muchachos deben haber venido para la boda, eh?"*

"What other boys? Waco said.

"Four of them. They wear Arizona State sweat-shirts. School chums?

"Butch Boyle," Sarah said with alarm.

"Yeah, yeah. Can we go," Waco said.

"Sure. *El amor no esperará."*

Sarah gunned the motor and jammed the gear shift into first. The ambulance took off with a lurch.

"You told that man we were getting married!"

"Yeah."

Sarah smiled. "That's sweet, even if it's not true."

Waco was now really worried. The *Le Belle* was a favorite place for college boys and that was probably where Butch and his buddies were headed.

Maria stepped back, grabbed the beer bottle off the bar and held it up threateningly. *"Maricon!"* she shouted. "You touch me and I kill you."

Butch stopped for a moment, then turned toward Juan, the owner.

"Señor, is this how you treat your customers?"

The fat man moved between Maria and the boy. *"Qué pasa*, Maria? This man, he is a customer."

"He is a pig, him and his rich boy friends," she shouted, trying to free her arm from the fat man's grip,

The other girls watched with blank expressions as the bartender looked to the young men. "I don't know what is wrong with this one," he said apologetically. "Why you no pick another one. They all the same, eh."

"Let her go. This could be fun," Butch Boyle said, winking at his friends. He pulled a large folding knife from his back pocket and slowly opened it.

Maria tried hard to not show her fear as the other bar girls gasped in shock and disbelief. Juan put up his hand. "Hold on there *amigo*. You can't do this..."

"Get out of my way or you'll get it too," Butch warned. "Get this asshole out of my way," he ordered his friends who did as commanded. One grabbed the bartender and the other two subdue Maria, knocking the beer bottle from her hand.

Butch stepped in front of her. His face was so close she could smell the stale beer on his hot breath.

"Let's see how your injun boyfriend likes you after I cut your face," Butch said.

Tears came to Maria's eyes as she struggled to get free. "You'll pay for this, *maricon!*"

Just then, a voice boomed from the entrance of the La Belle. "I believe the lady said she didn't care for your company."

Everyone looked over to the tall figure, silhouetted by the bright sun flooding through the open doors. Waco liked the way he sounded, like John Wayne. He opened his jean jacket revealing his grandfather's six-shooter tucked in his pants.

"Waco," Maria said, letting her arm relax as the boys loosened their grip on her.

Butch held his hand over his eyes to block the sunlight as he swaggered slowly toward Waco with the open knife at his side.

"I am a sworn deputy of Yuma county, and you must be Waco Lemuel. You are wanted for investigation of armed robbery..."

The other boys at the bar started moving slowly behind their leader, gathering courage in their numbers, only to stop short as another figure walked into the cantina. The sun glared off the double barrels of a shotgun.

"Your old man got no juice here Boyle. Back off!"

The fear and anger on Maria's face melted as she recognized Joe's voice. She hurried over to him.

The fat owner stepped between the two groups, holding up his hands. "*Muchachos, por favor*, no trouble in my place, please. You go back across the border and settle your problem. Okay?"

Maria took hold of Joe's arm. Her heart was pounding, but she was bursting with joy as tears now streamed down her face.

"You not so brave now," she shouted at Boyle.

"Go on, Joe," Waco said holding the old six shooter in his belt. "Get her outta here."

"You okay, partner?" Joe said.

Waco drew the six shooter and pointed at Boyle. "No sweat partner."

Joe started to back out of the cantina with Maria, holding the shotgun steadily in the direction of Butch's posse."

"Hey injun," Boyle shouted. "I ain't finished with you."

Joe turned around. "Don't worry white man. The time will come."

Waco waited until they disappeared into the blinding sunlight and then slowly backed his way toward the entrance..

"I wouldn't advise coming out too soon," he warned and slipped through the doorway, just like he'd seen on TV so many times.

Chapter Twenty-four

"You got no jurisdiction here,"
-Mexicn Border Guard

Maria was surprised to see Sarah behind the wheel of the ambulance, and even more surprised when she was greeted with a hug and kiss as she slide across the seat next to the her Joe jumped in next to her and slammed the door just as Waco came out of the La Belle and hopped in the rear.

"Let's go!" he shouted. "They'll be after us sure."

Sarah jammed the floor shift into first and the ambulance lurched forward. Joe stuck his hand out of the window and waved.

"Don't worry about the college boys. The won't be going nowhere for a while," Joe laughed.

"Wasn't that Bob and Rich Little Foot in the pick-up," Waco said, leaning over the front seat.

"Yeah, they took care of those dune buggies," Joe said. "Better avoid the border and take the back road to Mama's, Sar."

Maria took hold of his arm and squeezed it.

"You came back for me, *querido*. He smiled at her and moved to kiss her on the lips just as the ambulance hit a rut in the road and his lips ended up on her nose. They laughed.

The ambulance rolled through the back streets of San Luis, passing rows of small stucco houses, each surrounded by low fences where scrawny chickens busily pecked into the dry dirt in search of bugs, and an occasional goat strained at a rope that kept it from wondering off. The sun was well above the eastern horizon now, its hot rays beating through the windshield of the ambulance, forcing Sarah to hold one hand in front of her eyes as she struggled with the steering wheel with the other. The houses became fewer and further apart as they pulled onto the highway heading east, away from the border crossing.

Soon they were passing large lots of wreaked and rusting automobiles with signs in front of small shacks on the roadside advertising "*llantes, partes, junky.*" The horn from a pickup truck behind them blared as it pulled up next to the ambulance. A dark skinned man around twenty leaned out the window with long black hair waving in the air and a can of beer in his hand.

"Joe, brother," he yelled. "We got some business here. Catch up to you later, man..." The driver of the pickup stepped on the gas, and the truck pulled out in front of the ambulance. Little Foot waved and gave a out a loud, "Eeeeehaaaaa..." as the truck disappeared in a cloud of dust down a dirt road.

"I thought those guys were in jail," Waco said, leaning between Maria and Joe.

"Just got out two days ago," Joe said. "Ran into them after grandpop told me this crazy woman of mine run off."

Maria affectionately hit him on the shoulder. *"Loco indio."*

"They was on their way down here and said they'd help me out. Guess they're back in business again."

"What kind of business?" Sarah asked, keeping her eyes on the road .

Waco laughed and stroked her hair. "Sarah, how could you live around here all your life and not know what the Little Foots do?"

"Well, I don't," she said defensively.

"They steal cars," Joe said. "They steal them in the States, then bring them down here where they strip them and sell the parts. It's a good deal if you don't get caught. Kind of redistributing the wealth, you know."

"Sure," Waco added. "The people get their car stolen collect from the insurance companies, and the people down here make a living and keep their cars running."

"Helps the economy of both countries," Joe laughed. Maria hit Joe on the arm again. "You guys..."

"It's against the law," Sarah said, and they all laughed.

Waco leaned over and kissed her on the cheek, "And robbing dude ranches is blessed by the church."

"That was different," Sarah said coldly, even though she pressed her cheek against Waco's moist lips and a smile crept across her face.

By the time the ambulance rounded the road block which closed the washed out road leading to Norte del Sur, Mexico, the late morning sun was beating down on the metal hull of the ambulance, raising the temperature inside to 120 degrees. Joe had taken over at the wheel, gearing down from second to first and then into the compound gear as they bounced up and down through ruts and potholes in the road. Maria continued to hug Joe's arm, as if afraid if she let go he would disappear from her again. Waco had fallen asleep in the back with his head on Sarah's lap. She lovingly ran her hand through his sweat soaked hair.

"Norte del Sur border crossing," Joe announced, jarring Waco awake. "Mama Lo's, next stop."

"Better stop at my place first," Maria said.

"What for?"

"She's right, Joe." Sarah added. " We can't be seen from the border that way. No sense taking any chances."

He shrugged his shoulders and steered the ambulance toward the row of small adobe buildings along the dirt road, pulling behind the one where he had spent several romantic nights. He turned off the engine and a comforting quiet filled the hot air. They all sat in the ambulance for a minute, allowing the stillness to sink in and melt away the steady grinding of the motor and bumpy ride that had enveloped them for the last three hours. Finally, Maria kissed Joe on the cheek and slid across the seat, opened the door and stepped into the white heat of the desert sun. "I bet you guys could use a beer."

Waco's eyes popped open. "Did I hear beer?" he said sitting up He had been awake, but was enjoying Sarah's loving attention so much he pretended to stay asleep. But even the comfort of her affections couldn't replace the suggestion of a cold beer in the sweltering heat of the late morning desert. .

Joe looked over the seat at him. "You heard right, partner."

Sarah pushed Waco's hat down over his eyes. "You...I thought you were asleep..."

He pulled the hat back up onto his head and pulled her face to his. She didn't resist as his lips clung to hers. "I love you Sar," he said softly. "But right now I need a beer."

"Jerk," she said.

Waco and Joe smiled at each other as the two girls went into the small kitchen, giggling and talking. Waco switched on the TV, and then dropped down onto the couch along side his friend. An old western movie came on the black and white screen; the sounds of gunshots rang through the house as a cavalry and Indian fight stampeded across the nineteen inch screen.

Sarah and Maria came out of the kitchen, each holding two bottles of Mexicali beer. They squeezed in between the two boys and sat down.

"I love the way you've done the place ," Sarah said.

"It's nothing," Maria answered.

"Quiet," Waco said, taking the beer from Sarah.

"It's Fort Apache. John Wayne, Henry Fonda.... great flick."

"It bull," Joe said.

"It's a classic," Waco insisted.

Just then Jesus burst in through the door. "Where you guys been?" he said gasping for air. "Man, they got an army waiting for you guys at the border..." He stopped and saw his sister, and a smile of happiness crossed his face. "Man, *Capitán* Pedro is at Mama's, drinking tequila, and he's pissed man," the boy said.

Waco jumped out of his seat and put his hand on the revolver in his belt.

"Well, if this is it," Joe said hesitatingly, picking his shotgun off the table.

"Wait a second," Sarah said. "Are you guys crazy...?"

"*Pendejos,*" Maria shouted. "Let's see what is happening before you run off playing Pancho Villa."

"Screw it," Waco said.

"Maria's right," Sarah said. "I ain't losing you now, you fool. Let me and Maria find out what's going on before you guys go playing cowboy movies."

"She's right," Joe said. "Ain't no sense in getting crazy." He stood up and put his hand on Waco's shoulder. 'Come on, man. Let's cool it. They can't bother us on this side of the border."

Waco frowned. "Okay. I guess you're right. 'Sides, I ain't finished my beer."

"They got nothing on us, anyways," Joe said. He turned to Maria and put his hands on her shoulders. "You go and talk with Pedro. See what the story is."

"I'll go with her," Sarah said.

"Better not. Perhaps they look for you also." Maria said. She hugged Sarah, and then she put her arm around Jesus. "Come *hermanito*. We go together."

They watched quietly as Maria and the boy walked out the door into the white heat of the day. Sarah took Waco's hand.

Mama Lo's eyes lit up when she saw Maria come through the swinging doors. She hurried from behind the bar, shuffling her feet and catching the girl up in an embrace.

"Mi hija," she said. "I know you come back I know you no go back to that bad life."

Maria managed to break from the old woman's fat arms. She saw the Mexican Border guard, *Capitán* Pedro, sitting with his head on the bar, his hands clutching a half empty bottle of tequila. A deck of old cards lay strewn around the bar in front of him, and he was mumbling to himself.

Mama Lo took her by the hands. "You no worry, Maria. You see, Joe, he come back soon. He love you."

Maria whispered, keeping her eyes on the guard. "Joe is back. He came and got me; him and Waco and Sarah."

"Back?" the old woman whispered. "*Mamacita.*" She took the girl and led her through the back into the kitchen. "Where is my Jesus?"

"Watching the front," Maria said. "What is he doing here?" she nodded toward the door leading back into the restaurant.

"The *cabron*. He's been here for more than two hours. This morning, when I go out to collect the eggs, you know, like I do every morning, well, a see him and Senior Cassidy. They are playing cards like they do every morning. Then I hear this noise. It is sirens, and a cloud of dust comes up from down the road from Norte del Sur, and then I see these cars. *Policía*. It was like when Pancho was here and the *gringo* Army come to get him. You know. *Dios mio*, I say. They coming for my Waco and Joe, you know. But they stop at the border. I see Deputy Hank and this fat man in a funny green jacket get out and they talk with Señior Cassidy and the *cabron* what's sleeping in my bar in there. Then Pedro start arguing and yelling with them, and finally he grabs the cards up from the table and he come here. He tells to me, 'tequila,' and starts to drink. He say he was just about to have gin and those *gringos* ruined his game. Why he want tequila when he have gin, I don't know. Anyway, he get drunk real fast, mumbling how the *gringos* want him to do their job, and he no going to do it for them. He been here all morning."

Just then they heard voices from the front, and Jesus ran in through the rear door.

"It's Deputy Hank!"

"You got no jurisdiction here," they heard Pedro's voice from the bar.

"They sent me to see what's going on, Pedro. Come on man, *no problema, sí.*"

"You got no business in Mexico, Hank. Man, I had gin, and you guys messed it up. You got no jurisdiction."

"I just want a word with Mama," Hank said.

"Okay, Hank. But you got no jurisdiction see."

Maria moved over to Mama Lo, standing next to her as the tall deputy entered the kitchen. He tipped his hat, took a handkerchief from his pocket and mopped his face.

"Hot one," he said and then moved past them and went to the rear door, gently moving Jesus aside. He looked down the row of small back yards, and saw the ambulance. He turned back to the women.

"What are you going to do?" Maria asked.

"You leave the *muchachos* alone," Mama Lo added. "They no do nothing."

Hank smiled, and put his handkerchief back in his rear pocket. "Don't worry. They won't come across the border. If you see Waco and Joe tell them to wait until sundown, and then to take Bandido Road back across the border if they return to Norte del Sur. The Sheriff don't know that road."

Maria smiled. "Then you no going to turn them in, Hank?"

The deputy smiled back. "Me? I didn't see nothing." He turned and started to walk back into the bar. Then he stopped and turned back to them. "Tell them if they have to come back to be careful. The Sheriff is out to get them." He tipped his hat again, and then went back into the bar where they heard him say, "*Gracias* Pedro. Nothing here."

"You tell that new Sheriff, he no have jurisdiction in Mexico. You tell him he messed up my card game."

Chapter Twenty-five

"Man, you're the chief now."
                    -Richard Little Foot

Joe guided the ambulance through the blue-gray of desert twilight over the same road he had traveled the night before. Sarah was settled under Waco's arm as the two sat quietly bouncing up and down and to and fro in sympathy with the ruts and holes of the ancient dirt road that had been cut decades before by Poncho Villa's marauding army —thus the name "Bandido Road"— only now a new breed of bandit made use of the secret passage between Mexico and the U.S. These were not men crossing to the U.S. side of the border in efforts to sustain a war to liberate the poor of Mexico as Villa had, but the "coyote" who smuggled illegals across the invisible line that separated unemployment and poverty from the promise of jobs and money—the *coyote* who extracted thousands of dollars from poor peasants as the fee for deliverance into the promised land. The horse tracks of Villa's revolutionary soldiers had long since given way to the deep tire ruts from pickups and vans, and the bold incursions of the peasant army had now deteriorated into the clandestine smuggling of frightened peasants. And now it was passage for three fugitives from the Yuma law.

"Don't worry," he told Maria before they left. "I am chief now, and you will be my princess." But he knew that she saw the doubt in his eyes, although she would never question his decision to return to Norte del Sur with Sarah and Waco. She had drawn close to him and place his hand on her breast. "We act like nothing happened," and then kissed him hard on his lips as if trying to hold him there.

Sarah said suddenly. "They got no proof against us."

"Sure," Waco said, leaning across the girl and directing his comment to Joe. "They got no proof. You said so."

"They don't need proof," Joe said calmly, keeping his eyes glued to the road. "It's political now, man. They don't need no proof ."

"Sure they do. They can't just throw us in jail with no proof," Sarah insisted. "This is America."

Joe laughed.

Waco slumped down in his seat. "Yeah, but this is Yuma County, and Rowdy Boyle is America here."

"Say, what's that on the hilltop?' Joe said. "Behind us."

Waco stuck his head out the window just as a crack from a rifle shot echoed along the low hills that banked the road, and they heard the dull thud of a bullet against the side of the ambulance.

"Shit!" Joe said. "Where'd that come from?"

Waco pushed Sarah's head down. "There," he pointed toward the low hills to his right where a lone figure sat astride a dune buggy silhouetted by the full moon.

Sarah stuck her head back up. "What's going on!"

Another flash, followed by another crack from a rifle pierced the dark. Joe and Waco ducked down. Waco pushed Sarah's head down again as the bullet whistled through the open window of the ambulance and smashed into the windshield, leaving a small hole surrounded by tiny cracks. Joe stamped his foot on the throttle and jammed the gear into second, sending the big tires squealing around in the dust.

Sarah and Waco looked up just as four dune buggies appeared over the hill and sped toward them, kicking up clouds of dust into the darkening sky.

The low gears of the ambulance finally forced the tires to grip the dirt and it jumped forward. They heard the high pitched crackle of rifle fire over the roar of the ambulance's rusty muffler and the thud of the bullets as they ripped into the rear doors.

Waco reached for the revolver he had tucked in his belt, but couldn't move his arm because Sarah held it in a iron grip as they bounced violently around. He finally managed to lean his head out of the window to see four dune buggies closing in around them.

"The depot's just ahead," Joe shouted, pointing to the old train stop. "Let's see how those buggies handle railroad tracks."

He swung the ambulance off the dirt road, past several decaying wooden buildings and into the railroad yard where lines of rusty tracks headed nowhere into the desert.

The dune buggies skidded around behind them with their headlights cutting through the dark blue of the evening.

Joe shoved the gear shift into third, and the ambulance bounced up onto the track and banged down the train tracks.

Sarah held onto Waco with both hands to keep from smashing into the flat dashboard or into the roof. Waco spotted one of the dune buggies in the side view mirror just as it seemed to get locked into the railing, and then flipped over.

"One down," he shouted.

But Joe was more concerned with another dune buggy that was pulling along the driver's side of the ambulance. For a split second his eyes met the rider; it was Butch Boyle. Joe pulled the wheel of the ambulance hard to the left. The big tires bounced over the rail, forcing the buggy to turn sharply in order to avoid a collision. Joe ground the gears down to second and took out after the dune buggy— "I want that son-of-a bit..." his voice was swallowed up by the roar of the two vehicles' engines.

The two remaining buggies stayed hot on their tail as the ambulance roared after Boyle. Joe shifted into third again, gaining speed as the dune buggy headed for one of the dilapidated buildings with a decaying cattle car next to it.

"Joe!" Waco shouted. "You can't fit!"

But the warning came too late as the dune buggy shot between the building and the railroad car, and the ambulance tore after it, only to come to a jarring stop after leaving a trail of splintered wood and a horrible screeching. The ambulance came to a jerking halt as it lodged between the building and the side of the cattle car. For moment there was a deathly silence.

Then two dune buggies roared up behind them, followed by the third one that had flipped over. They were trapped. The doors were lodged against the building and the railroad car. There was no where to go.

"Get the hell out of there. You're under arrest."

Joe banged his hands down on the steering wheel. "Damnit!"

"Well partner," Waco said, wiping the sweat from the brim of his hat. "Look's like they got us."

"What will they do?" Sarah said, her voice trembling. "They won't hurt us?"

Waco put his arm around her. "Naw, they ain't going to do nothing. Right Joe?"

Joe looked at Sarah who was biting her lower lip, as if she was holding back tears. "Waco's right. They won't do nothing. They got us and that's all."

But Sarah could see the fear in his eyes.

"You mean you're going to let them take us alive?" a voice came from the back. The small brown face of Jesus peeked up from under a piece of canvas.

"What the hell you doing here," Waco said. "Damnit, we got enough troubles kid."

Just then there was a sharp banging on the back doors of the Ambulance and a voice demanding them to come out with their hands up.

Waco shoved Jesus' head down. "Get under that canvas and shutup. Then get home when it's all clear and tell Maria."

"Ah man,.."

"Shut up and do it!" Sarah shouted, her voice deep and mature. "This is serious."

Waco and Joe looked at each other with resignation. "Shall we," Waco said, sticking the revolver into his boot.

"Waco..." Sarah said.

"Just in case."

"After you," Joe said.

Waco helped Sarah over the seat into the back, and then swung his long legs over the seat. Joe followed behind them. They slowly opened the rear doors and were blinded by the piercing headlights from the dune buggies. Sarah held her hand over her eyes.

"Hold it there," a young sounding voice came out of the glare.

"Don't worry partner, we ain't going nowheres," Joe said.

They climbed out through the back doors to face the three boys standing in front of them. The one in the middle was a pimply faced kid who held a small automatic pistol. His hand was shaking. The other two boys held rifles. Sarah recognized them from the Pass Time.

"What are you guys doing?" Sarah burst out. "You

better not hurt us or...."

Just then Butch came roaring around the amulance and skidded to a stop, sending up a small dust storm. he. Everyone's eyes turned to the hulky boy as he dismounted the dune buggy and swaggered toward them, with a 12 gage shotgun.

"Well, well well, what have we here." He held the shotgun menacingly. "The bandits from Norte del Sur."

The other three boys backed off, grateful that their leader was there to take charge.

"They don't look so tough, to me." Butch laughed, walking up to Joe. "And if it isn't my old friend, the injun."

Before Joe could say anything Butch jammed the butt of the rifle into his stomach, buckling him over in pain. He dropped to his knees holding his midsection retching. Butch bashed him in the back of the head, sending him flat on the ground. He didn't move.

"You son of a...." Waco shouted as he started to reach for the gun in his boot. But Sarah grabbed his arm and restrained him.

"No Waco!"

Boyle stepped over to them. "So, you want to help your injun buddy, eh?"

Waco just stared at him.

"You coward," Sarah shouted.

"Shut up bitch," Boyle spit out, and slapped her across the face with an open hand.

Waco lurched at him only to meet the butt of the shotgun in his face, sending him reeling backward.

It was all Sarah could take. Her fear turned to outrage and she jumped on Boyle, clawing and kicking.

The hulking boy was taken by surprise as Sarah's fury. He tried to ward off her flailing hands. "Hey, get this crazy bitch off me," he shouted.

Two of the other boys rushed up and grabbed Sarah, pulling her off, but not until she was able to dig her nails across Butch's face, leaving a trail of blood. Boyle walked up to her, holding his hand to his cheek. Blood dripped between his fingers.

"I'll kill you, you bastard," Sarah yelled.

"A little tigress," he smirked, looking at his hand.

Sarah spit in his face.

"You little bitch," he shouted, and again slapped her hard in the face. A trickle of blood came out of the side of her mouth. Then he looked her over and smiled as he wiped his bloody hand of her shirt, and then squeezed her breast. "Nice tits," he smirked. "You guys wanta see them?"

Sarah looked back where Waco was trying to stand up, blood running down his face from a gash in his head.

"Sarah..." he glanced over at Joe who remained still on the ground, and then reached back for the pistol in his boot. It was gone.

"No Waco..." Sarah managed to say.

Butch turned to him and pointed the shot gun at his head. "I wouldn't be trying anything cowboy."

Waco slouched back to his knees, and looked on helplessly as Butch turned back to Sarah.

"Now, where was I..." he said. He grabbed her shirt and tore it open exposing her bra.

The other boys gawked at her exposed torso. Tears

came to her eyes. She had never felt so helpless and resigned herself to the worst.

"Come on Butch, I don't think we oughta..." the pimple faced boy protested.

""Shut up!" Butch shouted. "The bitch is going to get it," he went to grab at her bra.

"I wouldn't be doing that if I were you," a voice came out from the darkness.

Boyle and his buddies looked round. They saw a lone man standing in the shadows.

"What if I don't like your suggestion injun?" Boyle said.

Then they heard the metallic cocking of a number of rifles as about ten other Indian youths stepped into the light, each holding a weapon aimed at the boys.

"Then maybe we have Custer's last stand all over again," the man said, stepping into the light.

Boyle's buddies looked at each other, and then slowly dropped their rifles on the ground. The two holding Sarah let her go, and she rushed to Waco, helping him to stand.

Seeing his friends abandoning him Butch dropped his rifle. "You guys know we're authorized deputies of Yuma County. This could mean a lot of trouble for you."

Richard Little Foot walked up to Boyle. "Man, Indians are always in trouble. I ain't never signed no peace treaty with you people." He knelt down to Joe. "You okay, Chief?"

Joe smiled through pain. "Man, am I glad to see your ugly face."

"Yeah, well we said we'd catch up to you. Man,

you're the chief now."

Joe looked up at the hills where the moon was just rising, casting a magical blue light over the desert. He saw a man on a horse in the distance. It was only a shadow, but he could make out the flowing headdress and the rifle cradled in the man's arms—the Old Chief, overseeing his last battle.

"Kill the *caprons*! No prisoners."

Everone turned to see Jesus, standing at the open back doors of the ambulance, his dark brown face contorted in anger. Waco saw the fear spread over the faces of the college boys as the Indians fell quiet, as if considering the Mexican boy's demand. Then, one by one, the Indians began to laugh, and Richard Little Foot gave out a blood curdling cry, so the college boys weren't sure what was in store for them.

"What are you going to do with them. Rich?," Joe asked quietly. "This punk's pretty important."

Richard Little Foot's thick arm wrapped around Joe's waist, and he helped him toward the ambulance, laughing. "Don't worry, Chief. We'll just have a little fun with them. Hey man, this ain't no bullshit cowboy and Indian flick. We ain't crazy."

Waco found his pistol lying in the dirt near where he had fallen. He and Sarah limped behind Joe and Little Foot toward the ambulance.

"Well, not that crazy, anyway," Richard said, laughing again. He helped Joe slide into the rear of the ambulance with Jesus' help. Then he helped Sarah and Waco in.

"Thanks brother," Waco said.

Joe lay down in the back on the pile of blankets,

while Waco climbed into the driver's seat. He started up the engine as the rear doors slammed shut.

"Is he okay?" Waco shouted over the roar of the motor to Sarah in the back,

"I think so. Let's get out of here"

"I'm okay," Joe said weakly.

"We should have killed the *caprons,*" Jesus added.

"Shut up, will you," Sarah scolded, as Waco ground the gears into reverse, and the ambulance worked its way out from between the railroad car and the building, ripping more timber as it went. He slid the gear into first and headed into the darkness on Bandido Road toward Norte del Sur.

Chapter
Twenty-six

"Peyote, underwear? I told that damn Rowdy not to make me deputize them..."

-Sheriff Morrison

The border patrol agent had to adjust his binoculars. The rising sun made it hard to see the four silhouettes in the distance It looked like four young men standing on the rise waving their arms at him. They were in their underwear. *What the hell are those guys doing?* he asked himself. He steered his van in their direction.

The big guy, who seemed to be the leader, was ranting and the agent thought they must all be high on drugs.

He had seen it before; college kids eating peyote buttons and howling at the moon. The big kid insisted he and his companions were deputy sheriffs and that they had been attacked by a band of Indians. It confirmed his suspicions. He finally told the boy to shut up. Butch did as he was told.

The officer pulled a water bottle from his van and handed it to him.

"Here. Pass it around and then I'll take you in."

Butch took a long drink and then handed the bottle to the pimple faced kid behind him.

"You kids better get in the van and I'll take you into Yuma."

"No! We have to go to Nortre del Sur. Give us some guns and we can catch after those sons for bitches. They are fugitives from the Yuma Sheriffs Department," Butch said.

"The pimple faced kid stepped up. "Not me. I've had enough of this. I just want to go home."

The other two boys nodded agreement. "Come on Butch, this thing ain't worth it."

"Don't punk out on me guys," Butch said. Come on officer. We can still catch them."

"Sure, sure, Kid. But you have to admit. your story is pretty out there. Now, don't you think you ought to get some clothes before you go hunting down Indians?"

Morrison was just getting out of bed when the phone rang It was Agent Thad Tracer at the Border Patrol Office in downtown Yuma.

"We got a guy here says he's Rowdy Boyle's kid. Names Butch," Agent Tracer said. "You know him?"

Morrison hesitated for a moment, trying to gather his thoughts. "Yeah, what's he doing there?"

"Damnedest thing, one of our guys picked him and three of his buddies up in the desert wondering around in their underwear. Claimed he was a deputy of yours and had been attacked by wild Indians. My guy figures peyote."

"Oh shit. Why you calling me?"

"Tried to get hold of Boyle but couldn't trace him down. No one seems to know where he is." Tracer said. "You'd better come down here and pick him up."

Peyote, underwear? I told that damn Rowdy not to make me deputize them, Morrison thought. "I'll be there in a few minutes." He slammed the phone down. "Now I'm a godamn babysitter."

"For god's sake," Morrison said. "He's still in his underwear. Couldn't you at least find him some pants?"

Butch sat at a desk in an inner office with his feet up like he owned the place. He failed to notice Morrison's entrence.

"Hold on there now, Sheriff." Agent Tracer said. "It ain't like we didn't offer him some clothes. He has refused to cooperate with us. Says he'll have us all fired for not pursuing some gang of outlaws. Maybe you know what he's talking about."

Damn, he and his boys must have run into that gang from Norte del Sur, Morrison thought. "Where the other boys?" he asked.

"They got their parents to pick them up. They took the clothes we offered them. These kids...they're your deputies?"

"It's along story Agent."

"There you are Sheriff." Butch said, bursting out of the inner office. "Come on. We gotta get after them!" he started heading for the exit.

Morrison looked at Tracer and shrugged.

"Butch turned around. "My father's going to hear about the way you people refused to help me."

Agent Tracer smiled. "Sorry son, this is Federal jurisdiction. He turned to Morrison. "His father really Rowdy Boyle?"

"Afraid so," Morrison said, and followed Butch out the front door..

Chapter Twenty-seven

"This ain't happening in my county"
-Rowdy Boyle

Sarah wiped the dry blood from Waco's forehead with a damp cloth. He winced. The uneven breathing of Joe sleeping in the front room drifted into the small bedroom It had been past twelve when they rolled into Norte del Sur. Luckily there had been a couple of vacant cabins. Everyone seemed to be asleep.

"Where's Jesus?"

"Don't talk," Sarah said in a soothing voice. "Jesus is keeping watch outside. You just lay down." She coaxed him onto the bed and lifted his feet up onto the white sheet, and then pulled his boots off.

Waco felt something new in her touch; a tenderness she hadn't had before; a surety. Her voice sounded soft and sensual. He felt her nimble fingers unbutton his shirt, and then she slid her hands over his bare chest.

You know, Waco, Maria's really nice. I never talked to her before. I misjudged her in a lot of ways. She told me a lot of things I never knew..." Her hands slide up behind his neck and she softly stroked his hair.

Waco opened his eyes and looked into her's. His pain seemed to fade away as a feeling of urgency swept through him. Her hair flowed over him, and she slowly pressed her lips to his.

"I want to make love with you, Waco."

He felt her hand drift along his jeans, caressing him in a new way which took his breath away. He reached up and nervously untied the knot in the front of her shirt where she had tied it together. She smiled as the shirt slowly opened. She slipped out of it and unhooked her bra. She again pressed her mouth to his, this time harder as she took his hand and placed it on her breast. Her lips parted, and they embraced as the bright blue light of the full moon flowed over their bodies.

Rowdy Boyle was awakened by a loud voice that echoed through the guest cottage. The early morning sun glared through the faded window shade and fell on the face of the woman sleeping soundly in the double bed; a soft snoring sound slipping from her smeared lipstick mouth. He looked at her face with the heavy makeup caked on her cheeks, faded rouge and smudged mascara framed by a mop of unruly bleached blond hair. Why did he risk his career for this woman he wondered. It was always the morning after he asked himself the same question. But he had been seeing her behind his wife's back for over ten years. He climbed out of the bed and walked to the window where he pulled the shade aside just enough to see what the commotion was.

What he saw was a scene he remembered from a million cop shows he'd watched on the late night movies, for there in the court yard of the Pass Time Tourist Cottages was a posse, fully armed, and hiding behind four sheriff's cars, surrounding an adjacent cabin. Standing between the posse and the cabin was Deputy Hudnal, holding his hands out between the cabin and the armed lawmen.

"'I won't be a party to this," Hank shouted. "I've known these kids all their lives."

"Stand aside, deputy."

Boyle could see Sheriff Morrison, hiding behind his car and shouting through a bullhorn.

"You are relieved of your duty, deputy, and you will be prosecuted for obstructing justice," Morrison's voice bellowed with an electronic ring.

A voice came from the cabin. "Get out of the way. Hank. If those bastards want a fight, we'll give them one."

Hank turned toward the cabin. "Waco. Don't be crazy kid. This thing gotta stop here and now before some one gets killed..."

"Forget it Hank. They want a shootout, we'll give 'em one."

"Throw out your guns and come out with your hands up," Morrison screamed over the bullhorn.

Hank turned back toward the posse. "Sheriff, you want a fight you gonna have to go through me first." He put his hand to the revolver in the holster on his hip.

"And us too, white man."

Boyle's eyes shifted to where the sound of the new voice was coming. He spotted six or seven Indians, hiding behind the other cabins and small trees surrounding the courtyard, rifles at the ready. The voice came from one of the Indians, a heavy set, dark skinned man with long black hair flowing over his shoulders.

"This ain't happening in my county," Boyle said to himself, grabbing his pants off the bed. He stumbled into them as he opened the door of the cabin. "Just hold it right there, Sheriff," he shouted as the glare of the morning sun hit his eyes. "Just hold on, damnit."

"What are you doing here?" Hank said.

Just than Butch jumped out from behind one of the sheriff's cars, still clad in nothing but his underware.

"No dad!"

Boyle groaned upon seeing his son with a shotgun in his hands and nearly naked.

"What the hell are you doing Butch? And where the hell are your clothes?"

"They took our clothes and smashed our bikes," the young Boyle shouted. "See! Let them fight it out…"

"Son, put down that gun," Hank said.

Boyle felt a wave of anger flush over him. He stepped out from the cabin into the hot sun.

Inside the other cabin Joe and Waco positioned themselves, guns at the ready. Sarah crouched in the corner holding back a protesting Jesus. "This ain't the movies," she kept saying to him. "This is for real."

"What the hell's Boyle doing here?" Waco said.

"No telling, but he'd better hold off that crazy kid of his or this thing could turn into a real shooting match," Joe said. "You sure that old revolver of yours works?"

Waco looked at his grandfather's gun, and then cocked the hammer. "If it comes to it, I'll blow that asshole's head off."

"Well, I ain't goin' start it, but I can't vouch for the Little Foots out there."

"Talk to them Joe," Sarah demanded. "They listen to you. This is crazy."

Waco saw the fear in her face.

"She's right, Joe. Maybe this ain't such a good idea," he said.

Meanwhile, Boyle had stepped out next to Hank, "Morrison, call off your boys," he shouted. "You're after the wrong guys."

Suddenly a shot rang out and the antenna of one of the sheriff cars exploded. Everyone ducked, except Hank who stood his ground and turned toward the cabin. "Joe, call your boys off before it's too late," he said just as Butch pulled the trigger of his shotgun and the blast shattered the window of the cabin. Hank pulled his revolver and knelt, pointing it at the half naked boy.

Joe and Waco hit the floor. Joe held his hand over

his face. Blood dripped between his fingers.

"Goddamnit," Waco shouted. "I'm going to kill that sonofabitch!"

"Hold it! Just hold it a second!"

Joe and Waco cautiously looked up through the shattered window. It was Sid who had appeared from the Pass Time with Suzie trailing behind him.

"What the hell's going on here?" Sid shouted. He walked past the Sheriff's cars and up to Butch. He yanked the rifle from the boy's hands. "You ain't shooting no one, son."

Boyle got up from the ground where he had dropped at the first shot. He walked over to Sid and Butch.

"Get outta the way, Sid," Richard Little Foot warned. "These white men want a war, we'll give'em one."

"Cool it, Rich!" Joe said, stepping out of the cabin with his rifle. Blood dripped from his forehead where the glass from the shotgun blast had hit him. "I'm Chief here, and you guys listen to me. We're going to hear what these white men have to say before we start a war."

"But Joe..." Richard Little Foot protested.

"I said cool out, man. I'm Chief now."

"The Indian lowered his smoking rifle.

Sid leaned toward Boyle. "I thought we had a deal. What's going on here?" he whispered.

Suzie looked at Butch. "Aren't you ashamed young man, out here in your underwear."

"Shutup you old bitch," the boy snapped back, only to be answered by his father's hand across his face.

A roar of approval and laughter came from from the Indians as they emerged from their hiding places with their guns in their hands.

Suzie turned to Sid. He called me old..." She started crying. He took her into his arms and held her.

"You apologize to the lady," Boyle demanded.

Butch mumbled something.

"Louder!" Boyle said.

"I apologize."

"Morrison, take my boy back to Yuma," Boyle ordered.

"But..." Morrison weakly protested.

"I gave you an order, Sheriff. That is if you want to
remain sheriff."

"Yes sir," Morrison said, and came out from behind
his car and took Butch's arm. "Come on kid, let's go.
It's all over."

"And get him some damn clothes for God's sake,"
Boyle said.

Waco stepped from the cabin, followed by Sarah
and Jesus as the Sheriff and deputies got back in their
cars and drove off, leaving behind a small dust storm
as they sped out of Norte del Sur.

Chapter Twenty-six

*"I'll watch over your town
from now on, Grandpa."*
-Waco

Hank took his eyes off the road and turned them on his new bride, admiring the way she looked in the low cut peasant blouse from Puerto Vallarta. Daisy was holding her hand up, smiling at the diamond on her third finger. She had looked at the ring with the same self-satisfied expression at least a hundred times since they had left Norte del Sur for their honeymoon. Everything had happened so quickly after the day of the showdown that he realized he hadn't fully explained to Daisy why he had rushed in that evening, grabbed her in his arms, kissed her passionately and declared they were getting married. He hadn't even stopped to think that she might say no, but she didn't and they were off, stopping in San Luis to get married, and then two weeks in Puerto Vallarta.

For the first time he realized that if it hadn't been for Rowdy Boyle and Sid, he would probably have been caught in a cross fire and be six feet under the Arizona desert instead of returning from his honeymoon. It was only after he had found out that when Sid had gone off to confront the Representative over the cutting off of the water that he and Boyle had struck a deal. Sid had given the Representative all promotional rights to Norte del Sur. Boyle promised to call off the sheriff, and see that the case was closed against the kids.

Daisy started leafing through the pages from the pile of Yuma Star newspapers he had insisted on buying when they drove into San Luis so he could catch up on what had happened since they left.

"Oh look honey," Daisy said, cutting into his thoughts. "It says here that Representative Boyle has introduced legislation naming Norte del Sur a historic landmark. Isn't that wonderful. Gee, that'll make business boom I bet. We better make arrangements to have the bar added on as soon as we get back. You see that you take care of that hon."

He smiled to himself and reached over and patted her on the thigh. She playfully slapped his hand,' "You nasty old man," she giggled, and then added, "Golly, that awful Tom Foley was found dead up north in his cabin."

"What else does it say?" Hank asked.

"Well, says the sheriff has closed the case on the

robberies around here now that Foley's dead. Says their investigation showed that the Foley gang was responsible for the whole thing. Here Hank...look." She shoved the paper under his nose.

The headline was in bold print;

Last Of The Desperados Found Dead
String Of Local Holdups Solved

His eyes dropped to the bottom of the page where he saw a large boxed advertisements

Hank threw the paper into the back seat and started laughing. "Well, I had my doubts in the past, but Rowdy Boyle's got my vote this election, even if he is a damn Republican."

"What's that, hon?" Daisy said.

"Nothin' baby. Nothin' at all."

Boyle wasn't anyone's fool. The first thing he did after Morrison and his posse left Norte del Sur was to shake Hank's hand, thanking him for his bravery in a dangerous situation. He then pulled him aside. "Look deputy," he said. "There's no doubt what that you oughta be sheriff in this here county of mine. It's like

I said before; politics. You understand partner. But I'll tell you what I'm goin' do. I want you to take an early retirement, and I'll see to it that you get full retirement pay...at sheriff's rate. How's 'bout it?"

For the first time Hank liked the Representative. He was talking like Sheriff Garrett. He was talking like a real Southern Arizona man.

He stopped in the central square of San Luis, and then turned left toward the southern highway to Norte del Sur, Mexico.

"Don't you want to go into Yuma?" Daisy said.

"Thought we'd have lunch at Mama Lo's."

"But I thought that road's been washed out?"

"We'll see."

He's hunch proved right. As they pulled onto the Norte del Sur highway they passed a large road crew.

"Looks like they're paving the road," he said as they passed the workmen. The smell of burning tar floated into the car.

"You never did tell me what happened in Norte del Sur, hon. Gee, it must have been something, what with all these changes."

Hank took a handkerchief from his pocket and wiped the sweat from his forehead. He smiled. "Happened? Well, nothing really. Guess you might say justice happened."

Daisy rolled up her window and switched on the air conditioner. "It's obvious you're not talking." She slide across the seat and put her hand between his legs, and gentle squeezed. "Whatever happened, I'm glad it did.

* * *

The old Mexican snapped the tops off the two bottles of Mexicali and set them in front of the young couple sitting at the bar. "Yes sir, I rode with Poncho Villa." he said with a wide grin exposing the gold teeth that filled his mouth. "During the hard times, when the Revolution was just beginning, General Villa hid out right here at Mama Lo's."

His eyes glanced at the Mama Lo hauling dishes of steaming "especial" dinners to the tables filled with tourists. He never asked why; he was just glad that she had asked him to come live with her and help at the restaurant.

"Jesus," she snapped. "Bring fresh water, quick."

The boy rushed from the kitchen with a tray of water glasses, sweat pouring from his forehead. He nearly tripping over several small children playing on the floor.

"*Cabron*," The boy muttered to himself. He placed the water on a table where an elderly couple was sitting.

"Graci ass..." the fat woman said. "Esto es agua?" She held the glass up to the boy.

"Sorry lady, I don't speak the English." He hurried back into the kitchen where Maria was busy cooking, and Joe was helping dish up the food.

"*Chingado*, I don't like this."

"You," Joe said, wiping the sweat from his face. "Is this any way for a chief to act, slinging hash?"

"Both of you shut up," Maria snapped. "Isn't this what you fought for. Now we make much money. We can get married, and you, *hermanito,* will be able to go to a good school."

"Married?" Joe exclaimed.

"School?" Jesus said

Just then Mama Lo hurried into the kitchen, sweat pouring from her dark face. "*Mamacita,* why do they ask for menus when they always order the *especial? Locos gringos.*" They all broke into laughter. Joe put his arm around Maria's slim waist and pulled her close to him,

Sid walked down from the graveyard. The hot noon sun beat down on his head, but it felt good. He had just returned from several days in Phoenix where he had spoken at the state legislature for the bill to make Norte del Sur an historic landmark. It was his town; not a ghost town, but a bustling community. A tanker truck from the Southern Arizona Water Company sat by the water tower, pumping its precious cargo into the heart of Norte del Sur. The street was filled with cars, campers and trailers. As he stepped onto the path that led to the Pass Time a full tourist bus rolled down the dusty street and stopped. The doors opened and the passengers piled out, greeted by Bertha and Fran Little feather in full Indian costume and holding rows of beaded jewelry draped over their arms.

"Welcome to Norte del Sur," he heard Bertha say. "The last authentic wild west town."

Inside the Pass Time Mattie and Suzie were busy behind the bar, filling mugs of foaming beer from the tap, and popping the caps off coke bottles for the dozens of tourists that crowded in. He slide behind the bar.

"Suzie, isn't the afternoon movie started," he said.

She kissed him on the cheek. "No time, Sid. Ain't watched TV for a couple of days," she said without taking her eyes from her business. "How'd the hearing go?"

"Was on the TV news. Didn't you see me?"

"No time, Sid," she said. "Been like this for three days now. Luke says we'll have to hire some kids from the reservation."

"Where's Luke?"

"In the back, counting the receipts. Oh, and Sid. I'm glad you're back," she smiled. "Maybe you and me could take a walk after things quiet down."

"Sure, I'd like that," he said.

He slipped into the back room where Luke was sitting at a small table with piles of cash in front of him.

"Damn Luke. Ain't seen that much loot in years, you know what I mean."

"Success Sid," Luke said without looking up. "Success. Just like you always said. How'd things go in Phoenix?"

"I was on TV. Didn't you see me?"

"No time, Sid. Too busy here, How'd it go?"

"Well, you know what I mean, Luke. With Boyle behind us, couldn't miss."

"Great," Luke said, his eyes glued to the piles of bills as he separated the ones, fives, tens and twenties. "Going to have to put up some more cabins. Oh, and a real swimming pool."

"Sure thing, Luke. Where the kids?"

"Sarah and Waco went into town for supplies. Boy Sid, we're making a bundle. Ol' Norte del Sur ain't seen this kinda dough since the railroad was here. Man, are we makin' a killing."

"Sure Luke. Think there's anything on the evening movie?"

"Movie? Hell, Sid, we got the Indian show tonight. Ain't no time for television."

Sid scratched his head. "Well, maybe we can all catch the Late Show." He opened the back door.

"Where you going, Sid?"

"Think I'll just take a walk, Luke. You know, check things out."

"Sid, be back by four. You're scheduled to lead a tour. You know, tell the folks 'bout old Sheriff Merkins and all. Spice it up."

"Sure Luke, just like in the movies." Sid turned and walked back into the bright sunshine.

He headed back for the path leading to the cemetery. He felt a terrible need to speak with his wife. "Success," he kept repeating as he walked up the low hill. "Success."

Sarah sat next to Waco as the truck turned onto the Norte del Sur turn off, past the sign "Road Work Ahead," and onto the new black top that covered the old dirt road. She may as well have been a mile away from him. They hadn't spoken since they left Yuma.

She had been holding it inside for several days, and she finally had to speak, and it all came out at once, like exhaling her breath after holding it for a long time.

"I'm not staying in Norte del Sur, Waco."

He kept his eyes on the road.

"I decided I want to go to college. There's more in the world than Norte del Sur," she said, her voice rambling as if trying to get it out all at once because holding it only hurt more. "I want to know what else there is, Waco. I mean, I'll be back in the summers to help, and I think I want to teach, and I can come back here and teach on the reservation."

It all sounded better that way, and at the time she believed what she was saying.

Waco turned to her. He had always known she would go away some day and maybe never come back. He knew no one came back if they could find something better outside Norte del Sur. And even if things didn't work out no one ever came back when they left. Not until now.

"I never left," he could hear his mother's words as she spoke to him in the dirty hotel room in Yuma just hours before. "I want to come home, Waco. We can get the ranch going again."

"You understand, don't you Waco," Sarah said, putting her hand on his arm. "I love you, Waco. That hasn't changed."

He smiled as he kept his eyes on the road to Norte del Sur. "Yes Sar. I know."

Waco walked between the grave stones and markers in the cemetery overlooking Norte de Sur. He had never thought about it before, but there among the dead lay the history of his town. He wandered up to the run down section everyone called "Boot Hill." These were some of the people that made up the history of Norte del Sur—the silver prospectors, the cowboys and railroad workers, the gamblers, prostitutes and outlaws. Waco brushed the dirt from one of the Boot Hill markers that was still legible.

Cock Eyed Jack
Rustler and Outlaw
Died in a gunfight with Sheriff Merkins
this day of Sept 8, 1918

He walked down to where his grandparents were buried and stared at the shiny new gravestone for a minute. Then he took out the box his Grandmother had left and placed his Grandfather's six shooter and badge on top of the medals, and then thought about it a moment, He took the badge back and clipped it to his shirt. "I think I'll hold on to this Grandpa." He dug a small hole in the freshly turned dirt of his Grandmother's grave and lay the box into it. "These belong here with you Sheriff," he said, and filled the hole in.

He looked back at Norte del Sur. It had come alive.

"I'll watch over your town from now on, Grandpa."

He knew he would never leave. Maybe Sarah would come back. Maybe not. But for Waco, Norte del Sur was as much a part of him as was his heart.

The Old Chief sat on his horse overlooking the familiar town of Norte del Sur—the ghost town he swore he would never enter. He smiled and thought to himself that perhaps the final victory was his.

He glanced at the new watch on his wrist that Representative Boyle had presented him two days before in front of the entire State Assembly. He didn't know why, but he didn't ask.

The sun was sinking into the west and the sky was turning a dark blue. A warm breeze kicked up small clouds of dust over the desert and a thunder storm gathered in the north with low rumblings in the distance. One hour's ride back to the reservation, in time for the Late Show.

THE AUTHOR

L.Z. Smith grew up in Southern California where he made many trips into Mexico and Arizona. He now resides in Northern California and has worked many years as a Labor Journalist.

He has college degrees in Latin American History and Creative Writing.

He has three daughters and four grandchildren.